The More the
MERRIER

The More the
MERRIER

An Amish Christmas Romance

Linda Byler

Good Books

New York, New York

THE MORE THE MERRIER

Good Books books may be purchased in bulk at special discounts for sales promotion, corporate gifts, fund-raising, or educational purposes. Special editions can also be created to specifications. For details, contact the Special Sales Department, Good Books, 307 West 36th Street, 11th Floor, New York, NY 10018 or info@skyhorsepublishing.com.

Good Books is an imprint of Skyhorse Publishing, Inc.®, a Delaware corporation.

Visit our website at www.goodbooks.com.

10 9 8 7 6 5 4 3 2 1

Library of Congress Cataloging-in-Publication Data is available on file.

ISBN: 978-1-68099-613-5
eBook ISBN: 978-1-68099-471-1

Cover design by Brian Peterson

Printed in the United States of America

Table of Contents

Chapter One

IT WASN'T THE FACT THAT SHE WAS LEFT alone after Eli died that was so hard. It was caring for eight children in 1931, those bleak years of the Great Depression, when neither hard work nor skillful financial management made much of a difference, seeing how there was no money to manage and no jobs to be had.

Sammy was the oldest, at sixteen years of age, hired out to Jonas Beiler over toward Strasburg, working on the farm from sunup to sundown. He was a strong, curly-haired youth with an outlook as sunny as possible considering his father's passing. So that left seven children for Annie to feed and clothe, and no matter what she did, life had turned into a scramble for survival.

A small woman with an abundance of thick brown hair, wide green eyes that held a shadow of sorrow, and a wide, full mouth compressed with the hardship of daily life, she mourned the loss of her husband and wondered what God meant by casting her in the role of widowhood. But still, she bowed her head and said, "Thy will be done." She kept the cows, but sold two of the pigs to pay the feed bill, and acquired twenty chickens and a sick calf that she nursed back to health. Suvilla and Enos, ages fifteen and thirteen, helped milk the cows by hand every morning and every evening, and helped lug the monstrous milk cans onto the low flatbed wagon and haul them to the end of the drive for the milkman. They cleaned cow stables, forked loose hay and straw, fed the chickens, and ate coffee soup and fried mush for breakfast, a lard sandwich for lunch, and potato soup for supper. Curly-haired and big-eyed, their cheeks blooming with pink color, the children shed a few stoic tears for their father, and then tried to go on with their lives. Everyone had to die at some point, some earlier than others. That fact didn't exactly make it easy to say goodbye to their father, but they did their best to accept the simple words of their mother: "His time was up."

Ephraim was eleven years old, solemn and wise, and he instructed the smaller children in the way of life and death, repeating the words of the minister from the funeral service. Ida was barely a year younger, and like twins, they spoke and thought alike, although she hung on to every word from his mouth, an adoring younger sister whose devotion to her brother bordered on worship.

Emma, Lydia, and Rebecca were often referred to as "the three little ones"—six, four, and nearly three years old with thick brown curls plastered severely into rolls along both sides of their heads, the heavy tresses pinned into coils in the back. They were young enough to accept without question the disappearance of their father, feeling only the small portion of grief God allows for little ones.

It had been six months and twenty days since his passing, Annie counted as she sat on the back stoop with the sound of children playing mingling with the wind in the maple trees, the clucking of the chickens, and distant barking of dogs. She was weary to the point of exhaustion. Early spring, the time of plowing, harrowing, and planting, had always taxed her strength, even when she had worked alongside Eli, his sturdy frame ahead of her walking behind the plow, the reins secured behind his back.

This year she had Sammy at home for a few weeks, but the work was still more than they could reasonably manage. The seed corn was bought on credit, which was a weight on her mind and shoulders. What if there was not enough to pay it back? She envisioned losing their home. Did people go to jail for unpaid debts? No, the church wouldn't allow it. She'd have to make a humiliating trip to see Amos Beiler, the deacon, but so be it.

She watched the three youngest race across the lawn, marveling at their strength and energy after the meager soup in their stomach. The potatoes were all gone, even the smallest one, wrinkled like an old man's face. They'd gone down cellar, broke off every sprout to ensure the potatoes' well-being, but they knew the supply would run out in April or May, and the new crop would not be ready to dig till August.

There were canned tomatoes, green beans, pole limas, and corn left, but none of those vegetables satisfied hunger like solid, starchy potatoes. Cornmeal was good, though, and she roasted one ear of corn after another. She filled the oven of the solid range with the heavy ears of corn and allowed the odor of it to fill her with fresh hope. As long as they had roasted, ground cornmeal, they wouldn't starve.

The sun's rays slanted between the dancing maple leaves, creating a pattern of light and shadow. There was a blaze of color in the west, brilliant orange and timid yellow, a soft lavender that melded with the weightless blue of early spring. It was the kind of evening that made her feel as if everything was manageable. Possible. That she'd be all right in spite of the huge obstacles she faced. She leaned back, rested her weight on her elbows, stretched her feet, and watched a blur of small birds whirring across the sky in a frantic synchronized spiral of movement that took her breath away. Well, if God knew each sparrow that fell, and designed the ability of tiny birds to fly like that, then he would surely favor her with his kindness.

Yes. He would.

Dear Heavenly Father, guide me along this path you have prepared for me. Help me to make good choices, to protect my children. Give me strength for today.

She got to her feet. She was a small woman and wore the traditional purple dress with a black apron pinned around her narrow waist, her substantial white organdy head-covering revealing only a thin strip of her abundant hair and hiding most of her ears. She was a stalwart and modest figure that moved purposefully across the lawn, then bent to examine the rich dark soil for signs of onion tops pushing through. She straightened. Her eyes roved the perimeters of the yard searching for little ones, and, finding none of them, she turned toward the barn to come upon the three little girls on their hands and knees, poking a long hoe handle beneath the woodpile.

"He's in here. I saw him go," Lydia said excitedly.

A vague question of what was meant by "him" brought a smile to Annie's tired face. A mouse, rat, snake, earthworm? Which of God's creatures was hiding beneath that pile?

Suddenly there was a shriek from Lydia, a roar from Emma, a hurried scuttling followed by a mad dash in her direction. The smallest one, Rebecca, was toddling after them with howls of outrage. Annie brought her hands to her hips.

"Here, here," she said, speaking with authority. "Lydia, what is under the woodpile? Stop your *greishas*."

Small hands clutched at her side, her waist, tugged at her apron, with dusty shoes dancing around her own feet. She bent to scoop up Rebecca. "Shh. Shh. Hush."

"It's a snake. A black one as thick as your arm. It turned around and was going to bite us!"

"They don't bite, Lydia. Stop saying that. Snakes are good—they eat mice and rats."

She turned to go back to the house, the sturdy white dwelling with long, deep windows, a porch along the front, and a smokehouse off to the right. A cement sidewalk separated the green lawn like the part on the top of someone's head, with a Y that led to the smokehouse. Another block of cement contained the cast iron water pump with a tin cup attached to it, hanging on a piece of thick string. Everyone drank from the cup, without the benefit of even a weekly wash with the rest of the dishes in the house, so the handle was darkened by the repeated insertion of two fingers curled around it—fingers stained with soil, manure, tobacco leaves, hoe handles, and sweat.

A few yews grew in neatly trimmed rectangles along the front of the house, with a climbing rose attached to a trellis on the right. The windows were without light, the house as if everyone was remembering the loss of its owner, shrouded in grief. Never again would his joyous footsteps announce his arrival. Annie would never again turn from the cook stove to greet him, or walk with him to sit on the old davenport beneath the double windows in the kitchen. He had been taken from her by the freak accident that she had relived over and over in her mind—runaway horses that took a wagonload of firewood down a steep embankment. They'd uncovered his body by clawing at chunks of it, but his actual death had been by drowning, half in and half out of the icy Pequea Creek.

Annie herded her gaggle of little ones into the house, closed the door firmly against early spring night temperatures, then went to the cook stove to lift the round lid from the glossy top, before bending to grab a stick of firewood to keep the red coals from dying into the bed of cold gray ashes. She smiled to herself as three little ones tucked their feet under their skirts, leaning over the edge of the couch to make sure the black snake had not followed them inside.

One by one, the older children trickled into the house, fresh-faced and windblown, every one with a headful of thick brown hair in a variety of waves and curls, and wide green eyes that were always curious and full of life.

Ida and Ephraim were chattering like magpies, the words tumbling from their mouths punctuated by exclamation or giggles, eyes wide with disbelief or eyebrows lowered in concentration. They bent their backs simultaneously to untie the shoelaces on their high-topped leather shoes, peeled off their black cotton socks and stuffed them back into their shoes, then set them neatly in a row along the wall in back of the cook stove.

"Time for bare feet, Mam!" Ida trilled.

Bowa feesich. To be rid of cumbersome leather shoes, to wiggle toes and feel the delicious softness of grass and soil and pine needles, was a pure pleasure for all children between the ages of two and fourteen.

"No bare feet until you see the first bumblebee, Ida."

"Bumblebees have nothing to do with bare feet. Why do you always say that?"

Annie thought for a second. "I guess my mother said that, so I do, too."

Ephraim's round green eyes gazed into his mother's with no guile, pure and innocent as a forest pool. At eleven years of age, he was unusually quiet, reflective, a lover of school work and books. Annie lay awake at night considering how he hadn't shed one tear after the death of his father. While the remainder of the family allowed their sorrow to spill out at the funeral, Ephraim stood dry-eyed, his eyes unfocused, as if he had gone to another place that was happier.

"Ephraim, where were you?" she asked.

"Down by the creek."

"By yourself?"

"Yes."

"What were you doing there?"

"Watching the tadpoles."

Annie smiled at him, then turned to the stove again. She felt torn in so many directions since her husband's passing. With eight children and only one parent, how could there ever be enough of her time to meet each one's needs? For one moment, despair crept into her thoughts like an unwelcome virus, an annoying pain that she knew she must endure.

Each child was an individual, each one with her special personality, his own needs to be met, and Eli had been so good with the boys, such a strong leader, with clear and unflinching authority like a beacon of light to guide their feet. Yes, sometimes she thought he was too hard on them, and there were times when his words seemed suddenly harsh, catching them all off guard. But discipline was important for children, and he was carrying a lot of responsibility. The stress would get to anyone now and then.

Now he was gone.

Reality hit her repeatedly. Grief was a constant companion, an unwanted presence that sucked all the oxygen out of the atmosphere around her, often leaving her gasping for air, feeling numb and half-dead inside. It was for her children that she lifted her head from the pillow every morning, got through the dark days of winter. Now there was a promise of spring, with its bursting of new life; each blade of grass that sprouted was a harbinger of hope.

Taking a deep breath, she turned and spoke.

"Bedtime."

"We're hungry."

"There will be plenty of breakfast in the morning." She said it with confidence, but wondered how long children could stay healthy on coffee soup and fried mush.

The anxiety raised its visage once more, but she gave herself up to God's will, steeled against the fear, and spoke the necessary words.

"Ephraim, get the water ready."

She hoped her voice carried the proper authority. To get the water ready meant setting the agate dishpan on the bench by the back door, adding a good amount of cold water from the cast iron spigot in the kitchen sink, grabbing the teakettle that was always humming on back of the wood range, and dumping enough boiling water into it to produce a nice warm temperature for face washing before bedtime. With a wash rag that hung from a bed and a bar of lye soap, the night ritual was complete.

One by one, they bent over the soapy water, washed faces and hands, swallowed against the emptiness in their stomachs, and sat waiting till their mother produced the black prayer book, then turned to kneel at a kitchen chair. Who could tell what went through each child's mind as the soft voice of their mother replaced the deep, strong voice of their father, reciting the words of the old German prayer that had been written hundreds of years ago? Fluent in German, she read well, her voice rising and falling, comforting to the children's ears.

When they rose to their feet, she put the prayer book back on the shelf, sighed, and wished the children good night: "*Gute nacht, Kinna.*"

The children answered in unison before turning to wend their way up the staircase, their bare feet soundless on the wooden steps. The usual scuffling in the boys' room was followed by a scattering of voices, bedsprings creaking, a few footfalls in the girls' room. And then silence spread like a mist through the house.

This was the time Annie dreaded most, the long evenings that moved toward the stroke of midnight punctuated only by her soft sighs, whispered prayers, and shifting for a better, more restful position. This was when his absence felt as if someone had literally done her physical harm. A knife slash in her chest, a stray bullet grazing a section of her midriff, leaving a wound that wasn't deadly but one that would never heal.

She had loved so deeply. Eli had been the one she had always noticed, yearned for, as a youth. But she never thought he would acknowledge her presence, and certainly never want her for his wife. Tall, well built, too handsome for his own good, he'd broken a few silly girls' hearts before turning to the quiet, stone-faced Annie, bringing the smile to her lovely mouth, the glistening to her green eyes.

But as marriages go, theirs was not a perfect union. He was demanding of her physical love, and she the proverbial shrinking violet, needing her rest and the energy to feed yet another infant. He was robust, with a strong personality, a man who needed a social life, visiting friends, inviting them for an evening meal on a Sunday, going to barn raisings and livestock auctions, lingering at the local feed store to banter politics with "*die Englishy*," where Annie would have been content to stay home with the children.

Now, after his tragic accident, the house seemed lifeless, dead.

She had never realized the life he had breathed into his family's existence. Like fresh air and the light of the sun, his laughter had rung out through the rooms, fulfilling every child's need for a bit of merriment when times were hard. A good sense of humor quelled her worrying, effectively making her world a lighter place, so with his absence came the demons of her inability to cope with the hard task of providing for all of them. Occasionally she remembered the darker moments, when he would enter their home with a dark cloud over his head, barking orders and refusing to meet Annie's questioning eyes, but thinking of those times only brought a pang of guilt to her heart. She should have been more forgiving, quicker to meet his needs while she still had the chance.

The children were growing fast, thin and wiry, with seemingly bottomless stomachs. The milk check barely paid the bills, with two cows gone dry. The hay supply in the barn was alarmingly low, and it would be a few months before more could be cut. She would have to talk to Jonas Beiler, soon. He'd look for another hired boy even if she desperately needed the three dollars her eldest son brought home every week. She could not handle two freshening cows, the hay to be cut, the corn planting, not to mention the birthing of the sows.

Yes, she knew the Amish community would never let a widow and her children starve, of course, but she had her pride. There was no reason she could not carry on alone, even if it meant tightening their belts and sending the children to bed a little hungry.

Some days she had gathered dandelions and boiled the succulent new leaves in salted water. She put a bit of lard in the hot cast iron frying pan, stirred a cup of flour into it, watched it thicken, then added milk and the greens with a few hardboiled eggs stirred into the thick creaminess. Without bacon, it was bland, but the children said nothing, bending their heads and shoveling the life-giving food into their mouths with appreciation. Empty stomachs that have been in that state for too long can be easily filled, Annie reasoned. Soon there would be new onions and radishes, tender green lettuce to make creamed lettuce with onion and hardboiled egg. Meat was so low she could hardly remember cooking a large piece of beef or pork. To butcher a chicken meant the waning of her egg supply, and she needed the eggs to sell at the local grocery.

She'd have to send the boys to the creek soon. The trout would be hungry and she could make a fish stew. There were still dried navy beans in the cloth bag on the pantry floor, and flour. Salt, coffee, molasses, and cornmeal. Milk and eggs. The lard can had been emptied a few months ago, so she'd resorted to buying it, something she had never done while Eli was alive. There had always been the butchering of hogs, in the fall when the frost tinted the grass and days were filled with the winds of oncoming winter.

The weight of her responsibilities was crushing. She could have told the deacon in the church and received help, but it was not Annie's way. Stoic, long-suffering, and proud, she lay awake at night without the comfort others would readily have provided. She would keep the farm somehow, even if it meant sacrificing food and any earthly pleasures. Headed to the stairs, she caught sight of Emma's and Lydia's shoes, which seemed to mock her determination. They were much too small, and the soles were already separated from the shoe. Well, at least it was warm enough to go barefoot most days now.

Chapter Two

In the morning, after a deep sleep cut short by the harsh jangling of the windup alarm clock, things took on a new perspective as she made her way to the barn to milk, the translucent glow of the waning moon lighting her way. She got down the oil lantern from its wooden peg, set it on the board provided for this purpose, struck a match, tilted the glass chimney, turned the wick, and proceeded to light it. The small orange glow emitted enough light to see the seven cows in a neat row, tied to their stanchions, their tails swinging idly as they turned their heads to look at her with soft, liquid eyes.

She hung the lantern from a hook that swung from a heavy beam, grabbed the three-legged wooden milking stool and the heavy steel bucket, pushed on Marigold's hipbone, and sat down to milk. She tugged on the swollen teats after wiping them clean, then began the steady rhythmic squeezing of the front quarters, her hands clenching and unclenching as the milk flowed in thick streams, hitting the bottom of the bucket noisily.

Now where was that Enos? He knew the cows should be given their feed while she milked. It always kept them content. When Suvilla opened the cow stable door and let herself in, shivering, Annie asked where Enos was.

"He's not my responsibility," she answered sharply.

"Suvilla, I'm in the middle of milking. Go to the house to see where he is."

Without bothering to reply, she went, obeying her mother in spite of her reluctance.

Annie continued milking, working through the normal tiredness of her fingers till she had the first cow stripped clean of her milk. A blush of color appeared on her cheeks. She felt invigorated, ready to tackle any job, no matter how strenuous.

"Good morning, Enos, sleepyhead," she called out when he stumbled into the warmth of the cow stable.

He grinned sheepishly, stretched and yawned, then propped the palm of his hand on the rough wooden post that supported the heavy beams above them.

"I was tired."

"Well, you need to feed the cows, quickly. Bessie needs an extra half scoop, she's milking heavily since she calved, alright?"

He nodded and ambled off, his lanky frame already showing promise of being tall and strong.

The tinkling of streams of milk hitting the bottom of Suvilla's milk pail, accompanied by the rasping of the feed leaving the metal scoop, the pungent scent of cow manure, ground corn, and loose hay, the grinding of the cows' teeth, were all familiar sounds that held the promise of her world righting itself and settling comfortably on strongholds of hope. The long night with its talons of fear was a thing of the past.

Pleased to see the second galvanized steel milk can fill to the brim, she set the strainer aside, set the lid on top, and tapped it firmly in place with the rubber mallet. Then she helped Suvilla lift it into the cold water of the cement cooler. There would be five full cans to be rolled on the back of the wagon and taken to the end of the farm's drive for the milkman to pick up.

She cooked breakfast that morning with a song on her lips, whistling low under her breath as she boiled the strong coffee, sliced the congealed cooked corn mush into neat rectangles, and fried them in shimmering hot lard. Suvilla sliced bread from the high loaves and placed a slice in each soup bowl, only half a slice in the smaller children's bowls. Annie added milk and a bit of maple syrup to the coffee, then called the children to breakfast before flipping the slices of mush, standing back to avoid the needles of spraying lard.

Her mouth watered as she slid the pans to the middle of the stove, using her apron as a hot pad. She got down the hook to lift the round stovetop lid and reached for a few sticks of wood. The fire was dying down, and to fry mush properly you needed plenty of heat.

Rebecca was crying as she made her way down the stairs, her bare feet creating the uneven rhythm of a small child's descent. Annie had no time to comfort her, so she told Emma to go see what was wrong, then got down two plates to hold the golden rectangles of fried mush. She ladled the milky, sweet coffee grounds that had settled on the bottom of the kettle, then slid into her chair and bowed her head with her hands folded in her lap. The children followed suit without being told, lifting their heads after Annie lifted hers. The silent prayer was always a time of gratitude for what was placed before her, but it was also a time of discreet observation of each of her children's obedience or lack of it.

Suvilla used to be extremely devout, her head bent so far down that her chin grazed her thin chest, her eyes closed in concentration as her lips moved in prayer. Lately there were times when she seemed to not be praying at all, her head barely bowed. Beside her, Enos's eyes roved across the table, turning slightly to check the amount of wood in the wood box behind the stove, his thoughts very obviously not related to food in any way, while Ephraim was praying quite piously. The smaller children all bowed their heads, some more than others, but all were obedient to the unspoken rule of "patties down."

When Annie lifted her head, she had a clear view of the white barn. She blinked, then took the back of her hand to wipe her eyes, thinking the mist by the cow stable window was a blurry vision. A wisp of fog? But the morning was so clear, so painfully bright and lovely and windy.

There it was, though.

She half rose from her chair, her eyes wide.

"What is it, Mam?" Suvilla sked, her spoon halfway to her coffee soup.

"I'm not sure. Enos, look. Does it look like something is in front of the cow stable window?"

He turned halfway from his seat on the bench, then swung his legs over before getting to his feet, then hurried to the window.

"It . . . it looks like smoke?"

It was a question he already knew the answer to.

He was out the door without further words, Suvilla and Ephraim on his heels, followed by a white-faced Annie, running as best she could with the loose sole of her shoe flapping.

When Enos yanked the barn door open, it was the draft of air that gave vivid life to the smoldering flames that licked along the wick of the kerosene lantern they'd thought to be extinguished. The flame had crept along the glass after it had fallen from its precarious perch on the board along the wall, finally reaching the small tank and erupting into flame, flames that licked greedily at loose hay and dry boards, bits of sawdust and dried fabric feedbags. With no breeze, it burned lazily, cleanly, a line of low flames snaking out from the contained kerosene fire on the cemented walkway where the lantern had fallen.

The cows mooed now, tugged at the restraints, danced from foot to foot. Their eyes rolled in terror as the heavy smoke increased to a dense black cloud.

"Let the cows lose!" Annie screeched, her voice a roar above the crackling flames. She plunged directly into the stinking black smoke from the kerosene lamp, now fanned by the rush of cold wind that blew through the opened door.

The cows were panicked now, bawling and jerking back on the leather collars around their necks, their hips and legs swaying first to one side of their stalls, then another, trying in their own clumsy way to free themselves from the oncoming flames, which made it extremely difficult to loosen them.

Her eyes watering, coughing and gagging, Annie tried desperately to find an opening between the first two cows, but their agitation made it impossible. The moment a panicked cow felt a hand on her hip, she leaned into it, squeezing the limited amount of air from her already tortured lungs. She heard coughing, tried to cry out to Enos and Ephraim.

"Get out! Go back!" she screamed, now that she felt the immensity of the smoke's evil power.

She was awakened by a distant noise, someone calling her name. Immediately she found herself retching and heaving, giving in to the thick slime in her throat. Unable to open her eyes, the burning like a living worm encrusted with pinpoints, she lay on her back with tears from her squeezed eyelids creating tracks through her smoke-blackened face, gasping for breath, before turning to retch again.

"Mam, Mam!"

She heard the agonized cries from Suvilla and wanted to answer, but was overcome by wave after wave of crushing nausea. She was aware of Enos and Ephraim, wanted to raise a hand in protest, but could do nothing but turn her head and heave weakly into the cold, windblown grass.

Dan Beiler had gone to the small town of Intercourse to the hardware store known as Zimmerman's, having run out of two-penny nails when he was in the middle of remodeling his kettle house. His horse was feeling his oats, which was a nice way of putting it, he thought grimly, as he hung on to the reins and hauled back with all of his strength. He didn't know where the line between running away and merely running was drawn, but he knew this old hack he was driving didn't feel as if it would hold together too much longer, at this alarming rate of speed. After he had the creature under control, he decided the horse needed a longer run to rid him of all this excess energy, so took the long route between New Holland and Intercourse by way of Smoketown along the Old Philadelphia Pike, and allowed the crazy horse to stretch out and run until he played himself out.

He could see the billows of smoke even before he heard the fire alarms, tugged on the right rein, and turned onto the next road he figured would take him to the fire. Someone might need his help.

The farm was set back from the road, a clump of maple trees surrounding the two-story white farmhouse, a white barn that was in the throes of an evil fire licking at it from within, by all appearances. He had no idea whose residence it was, but he passed men on foot, drove into a field as fire engines screamed behind him, then hurriedly tied his lathered horse to a fence post and ran all the way to the fire.

On approaching the burning barn, hearing the agonized bawling of tethered animals, he remained reasonable, and stayed away. He was on his way to offer his services to the firemen instead when he found the small group on the grass behind the smokehouse, the terrified children grouped around a blackened person half sitting, half laying against the side. He could see she had been inside the burning building, as had the oldest children.

"Is she alright?" he asked, squatting beside her to look into her face.

Suvilla replied, coughing between words. Her hair was singed and her face streaked with black. "I think she got kicked, but we dragged her out. Somehow . . ."

She looked a little dazed. "Wow," Dan answered solemnly. "You saved your mother's life. Has a doctor been called?" He looked around, wondering why none of the firemen had come to help this woman.

Suvilla nodded, said someone was coming.

He looked at the woman's face, reached out to touch her shoulder as she opened her eyes. He was met with a depth of sorrow and suffering that spread through his soul.

"I'm alright, I think," she whispered.

And still she held the light in his eyes.

"Where is your husband?"

The three little girls were huddled on the ground with their mother, and spoke as one.

"He's in Heaven."

Dan nodded. Small, blackened, defeated, she was like a flower beaten by storms, stomped on and mangled. A great pity welled in him, an empathy that filled his chest until he couldn't speak. He merely bowed his head and allowed her pain to be his own. He knew exactly what she had gone through, was going through. He'd been down that road himself, only three years ago.

He steadied himself with a deep breath.

"Let's get you into the house."

She shook her head. "I can't walk."

He looked around, saw the flames, the exposed beams, the fire trucks, the crowd, heard the crackling and hissing. He asked the children to step aside, then slid one arm beneath her shoulders and another one beneath her knees and easily picked her up off the ground and carried her into the house, one arm dangling.

She protested quietly, but she was weeping, so words were difficult. He put her on the old davenport, pulled the green blinds, and told her to stay inside with the children. He instructed Suvilla in getting a hot bath for her mother, and how to fix a bracing cup of mint tea with milk and honey. When the doctor arrived, he left quietly, suddenly feeling out of place and useless.

The barn and all its contents were completely destroyed. The pigs in their pigsty and the twenty chickens in the henhouse survived. The horses were out to pasture and stayed there, but one of the wooden wagons parked in the haymow burned to the ground with the rest of the barn.

Dan Beiler went home to his children and told them the story of his almost runaway horse and the subsequent fire, the widow and her eight children. He could not get her image out of his mind—those sorrowful eyes that were the color of oak leaves beginning to turn.

He went to the barn raising when the whole place was swarming with women bringing copious amounts of simple food, burly men and skinny teenagers working side by side to erect a new barn for the widow and her eight children. When he was on the highest rafters he found himself trying to get a glimpse of her, but he saw only her children. Where was she? Was she still recovering from the smoke inhalation? Perhaps she was more seriously injured than he had thought. But surely the men would be speaking of it if that were the case. He wanted to ask, but he knew if he did, eyebrows would be raised immediately, and that was the last thing he wanted. A widow and a widower. Aha.

Dan thought back over his last three years of emptiness and grief. The first year had been like living in

a dense black cloud. His world had become a gray
landscape that contained only enough oxygen in the
atmosphere to keep him alive. His only reason for
living was his six children: Amos, Lavinia, Hannah,
Emma, Joel, and John, starting at age twelve and
continuing every other year except for Hannah and
Emma, born only a year apart.

He'd carried the vulnerability of self-blame for his
wife's death for too long. Pneumonia was common,
but some recovered. She had not. A long winter of
arnica, onion plasters, mustard plasters, comfrey tea,
kerosene and brown sugar, turpentine, pills from the
doctor that had given her relief for a few days, before
she fell victim to her agonized coughing, her lungs
full of infection and bacteria.

He had loved her with a quiet, gentle, undemand-
ing kind of love, a husband who made life a bit cozier
in hard times. The children knew nothing but a home
that was a safe haven with an atmosphere of harmony
and understanding, so when they were plunged into
a sea of grief and dreadful emptiness, Dan had his
work cut out for him, balancing the farm and his
bewildered children adrift in a new world.

Almost, he'd married Bertha Zook, a sweet woman who had been too busy caring for her ill parents to ever date or marry. Urged on by his family, stating the need to acquire a mother for his children, he tried to love her the way everyone was sure he would. They had sat together in her parents' kitchen, and he found her intelligent, well spoken, certainly with a loving heart. But something was missing, and after several months he decided it was wrong to drag the relationship on any longer. He knew for certain he was never going to ask for her hand in marriage, and so he told her that any man would be blessed to have a wife such as she, but that he was not ready to remarry, and that she should not wait for him.

Nothing stirred him emotionally as far as friendship with a woman went, so he was shocked to find himself thinking so much about the widow Annie.

Annie had, in fact, spent a few days in the hospital in Lancaster until her lungs cleared up. Her mother and sisters stayed with the children until she was well, and later cooked food for the barn raising. They had no doubt she'd be all right. The Amish community would band together to help her; a poor widow touched the hearts of everyone around her.

The church paid for the barn, her father provided cows, the sun warmed the earth and the rain replenished it. Potatoes and peas went into the soil, and sprouted in long green rows like small soldiers lined to attention. Annie could hardly grasp what the folks around her had done to help. It was almost too much. She had no choice but to let go of her pride and simply let the gratitude-filled tears flow. The morning of the fire became a painful blur in her memory. She pushed it aside, knowing if she dwelled on the horror of that day she'd never accomplish all the tasks at hand. Though she did sometimes wonder about the man who had carried her to the house. Or had she just imagined that? She had been in something of a delirium for those first twenty-four hours. But the voice . . . she remembered his calm, soothing voice so clearly. She could ask her children, who had miraculously been unscathed, but no, that would not be proper.

Chapter Three

THE SUN CONTINUED TO WARM THE SOIL OF Lancaster County through May and into June. Warm breezes that formed across the eastern shore danced their way into the mainland, bringing humidity and rain, enough to produce abundant pea vines, glorious cucumbers, and bush beans clumped so heavily, one hand rummaging among the leaves easily produced a fistful.

Sammy came home to live and work through the spring and early summer, which turned out to be an enormous help to Annie. He was a carefree spirit, laughed easily and often, took his father's death as a chastening from God, and went on with his life. He had a host of friends and ran around from home to home in an old roofless courting buggy with torn upholstery and a tricky lid with misaligned hinges on the box behind the seat. To see Sammy with his friends brought Annie a vague feeling of discontent, a bittersweet nostalgia of her own years of *rumschpringa*. At these moments, any little thing could produce tears of sorrow for her beloved Eli—a blooming rose, the sinking of the sun in its fiery glory, which brought a longing to sink along with it.

Life was hard. To greet company with a semblance of happiness, to pretend she was even vaguely interested in the voices around her, to answer when a question was asked, was sometimes more than she could accomplish. So when visitors came and went, they had good reason to be concerned.

"She looks bad," they said quietly to their husbands.

"Mark my words, she'll have a nervous breakdown."

"It's been almost a year, and I don't see much change."

"I pity those children with that *unbekimmat* mother."

As folks will do, they passed judgment without the necessary cushion of compassion, so Annie was perched on a hard pedestal in the view of surrounding friends and family, her face white and drawn, her contribution to conversation nearly nonexistent.

Didn't she appreciate the new barn and all the help that had put her back on her feet? She was like a sad dark shadow of her former self, and it was indeed high time she snapped out of it.

But they didn't know about the times they were not with the family. The times when her love for her children was like the cup that was filled to the brim and running over, supplying the sole reason for going on. It was the reason she worked from dawn to dusk, milking cows, driving the two-horse hitch in the wooden farm wagon, forking hay and cleaning stables. She chopped wood, heated water in the iron kettle, poured it into huge galvanized tubs, did her laundry with homemade lye soap, pegged it on the line, and was proud of the dazzling whites. She hoed in her garden, picked vegetables, and canned them in mason jars. Every bean and cucumber and tomato was preserved. So were the peppers and apples and watermelon rind and the corn and small potatoes. Red beets were pickled in their own juice, with sugar and salt and vinegar, a dark burgundy color that added variety to the green and yellow on the shelves down cellar.

The children all worked alongside their mother, and their childish banter lifted her above the grief that so easily consumed her. Her children were her life, all that she needed. The children and her faith in God, who sat on His throne in Heaven and directed their lives as He saw fit. "The Lord giveth and the Lord taketh away, blessed be the Name of the Lord." The Bible verse meant so much to her, was often whispered just under her breath as she turned the crank on the hand wringer, fed the worn cotton dresses and the patched underwear through the rollers, then rinsed them in hot vinegar water before starting the process all over again.

Her arms were like steel, her legs strong and muscular, yet she retained her womanly figure. She had no time to think about her appearance; she merely arose every morning, pulled on her dress, and pinned a gray apron around her sturdy waist. She combed and twisted her luxuriant hair into a tight coil on the back of her head, set the white covering over it, and faced the day.

It was hot. The heat shimmered across the hayfields like some strange dream, the scorching wind rustling the leaves on the stalks of corn, turning the children's faces a deep shade of brown. *Like little acorns*, Annie thought, as she watched them shrieking and tearing across the lawn, in pursuit of some unwilling barn cat. She smiled to herself, then. A smile that lifted only the corners of her eyes, but it was a beginning of the end of the debilitating grief.

She viewed the rows of bright jars on the can shelves in the cellar, the reward of days of backbreaking labor, and felt the smile deep inside of her. The rays of happiness were like the sun that only appeared occasionally, the scudding dark clouds of her grief obscuring it. Now, though, it seemed to happen frequently, and she knew the truth of her mother's words: "Time is a healer. This, too, shall pass."

Then one day she received a white envelope with no return address and masculine handwriting amongst the other mail. Annie took it silently from Emma and thanked God it had not been Suvilla who brought the mail in. She lifted her gray apron and discreetly put it in her dress pocket, then flipped through the other mail, opening the letter from her sister in Berks County.

She sat on a kitchen chair, the afternoon humidity building like a furnace in the house, wiped her face with the familiar square of muslin, and read the pages with enjoyment. She smiled, she frowned, she cried. She breathed deeply, shifted positions, then lowered the pages to her lap and stared into space.

Sarah thought she could move to Berks County and live alongside her and her husband. Life would not be quite as hard without that mortgage on her farm. Annie tried to imagine it. She loved her sister Sarah, knew without a doubt she would be a huge help, both emotionally and spiritually. And financially, for sure.

But the children. They were so well adjusted here on the farm, in the school, in the church.

She put the letter in her desk. Eli's desk, as she always thought of it. She turned and began to pour water into a bowl for a batch of bread. She'd have to think about it, discuss it with the children.

After everyone was upstairs, she stood in the middle of her kitchen, the oil lamp creating a yellow glow, the heat lingering long after the heat of the sun had disappeared. Her heart began the quickening thud of agitation. She exhaled sharply, then drew a deep breath to steady herself, before slowly retrieving the letter from the depth of her pocket. The thing had been like a rock, begging her to open it all day. It could have been from anyone, of course, but somehow she knew, the way women sometimes do, that there was something important about this particular letter. With fingers that were slightly unsteady, she tore a corner of the envelope, inserted one finger, and ran it along the seal.

It was one sheet of lined paper.

Dear Friend,

Greetings in Jesus' Name.

I was there with you when you experienced the tragedy of losing your barn. I am hoping your health has been restored.

My name is Daniel Beiler and I am a widower with six children. My wife, Sarah, passed away three years ago. She had pneumonia.

I have prayed at length, and still feel the same, so I am taking it as God's will for my life. Would you consider starting a friendship? I would like to know you better. If it is alright with you, would September the fifteenth be acceptable to meet?

You understand, it would be late, so the children are asleep.

Please honor me with a reply.

In Jesus' Name,
Daniel Beiler

Annie didn't know what to do, so she cried. She sobbed and hiccupped. All the pain of parting with Eli crashed down on her head like crumbling plaster. And then, as if that weren't enough, she felt a deep shame. For the fact was, she wanted a husband. She wanted to wake up in the morning with another warm human in the bed beside her, someone to talk to, to share her responsibilities, and yes, to touch, and to love, and to cherish the way she had cherished Eli. Surely it was too soon to want another man.

Another man . . . those words in her mind brought a fresh wave of tears.

Of course, there were the children to consider. What about Suvilla? Sammy? They were old enough to have a voice in this very serious matter. What would they think of their mother starting a friendship with someone new? Should she ask them, or was that improper? This was a whole new world to navigate. She wished there was someone trusted that she could seek out for guidance, but of course there wasn't. For a moment she wished she had the kind of mother she could turn to for advice, but that was simply not the kind of relationship they shared. Where Annie was sentimental, her mother was practical. Where Annie welled with emotion, empathy, deep feeling, her mother kept stone-faced, never shed a tear that Annie could remember. Annie often felt ashamed that she couldn't keep her own emotions better in check. She knew her mother disapproved of crying—but then, she disapproved of most things. Likely that came from Annie's grandmother—but she was the last person Annie wanted to think about now. She actually shivered, the image of her grandmother bringing with it a cold wave of anger, disgust, and then, just as quickly, guilt. She should respect her elders, she knew.

Her thoughts came back to the letter and she wept on. She cried until she felt ill, then laid her head on her folded arms atop the kitchen table and allowed all the anxiety and indecision to overwhelm her. She tried praying, but it felt like the silent pleas for wisdom and direction didn't make it past the ceiling. She felt alone, intimidated, undone.

Slowly her tears subsided, her breathing returned to normal. She lifted her head, wiped her eyes, blew her nose in the sodden handkerchief, then got up and threw it across the kitchen in disgust.

Six children. *Six!* She had enough to do with eight of her own. This whole thing was just ridiculous. Why was she obsessing over it? It was too soon since Eli's death, fourteen kids would surely put her over the edge of sanity, and she knew nothing about this Dan Beiler. He was probably just lonely and overwhelmed with all those children and wanted a *maud* that he didn't have to pay. She should just reply with a polite no and be done with it.

She remembered then, in spite of herself, the feeling of his strong arms carrying her into the house, the gentle voice he used in instructing the children in her care. So she hadn't imagined him. And apparently he'd been thinking of her ever since then.

She slept only a few hours that night and dreamt restless dreams that made no sense, leaving her with a vague sense of foreboding and a serious headache all morning.

The next day her mother came to help her pick green beans and cucumbers, wearing her stiff black bonnet and no shoes, her bare feet walking across stones, rough cement, and prickly grass as if she was wearing invisible shoes. Austere, a formidable figure complete with a high forehead and hawk-like features, the large green eyes missing nothing, she put Annie on the defensive immediately. Her greeting was short, clipped, and to the point, wasting no time on niceties, certainly no sympathy.

"No help unhitching?" she called from the washhouse door.

"Oh, Mam. Sorry. I didn't hear you pull in."

"How could you miss it?"

"I must have been in the back bedroom."

"No matter."

But Annie was left with the distinct feeling that it did matter very much. She sighed.

"The yard needs mowing." Coming from her mother, it was a rebuke more than an observation.

They walked together toward the house, her mother surveying everything she passed with a critical eye. Annie wished she'd had time to sweep the entryway, which she now saw had clumps of dirt, a stray feather one of the children must have found and then dropped on the floor. There were a few plates and a coffee mug in the kitchen sink.

"Sammy had to help out at Jonas Beiler's," she explained. "So that left the girls, and they were busy with the cleaning. We had four bushel of tomatoes to tend to."

"On Saturday?"

"Yes."

"You should have done them on Friday."

Annie had no energy to delve into a detailed account of Friday's work, so she said nothing.

"What's this?" Her mother's voice was curious and accusing at once.

Annie's heart took a nosedive. The letter. How could she have been careless enough to leave it out? Had any of the children seen it? Thank goodness they were now all outside and wouldn't hear whatever her mother was to say next.

Her mother's thin hand raked it from the desktop, her eyes following the obviously masculine curve of the handwriting. She read it quickly and then held it out in front of her, disgusted, as if it contained a forbidden fruit.

Annie swallowed. She clasped and unclasped her hands behind her back, watched in disbelief as her mother waved it angrily.

"You will not, Annie."

Annie nodded, felt as if she'd been caught in some unforgivable sin.

"Your husband is gone only seven months. Who is this man?"

"It's ten months, Mam."

"And you are receiving offers? Have you no shame?"

"Mam, it's only a letter. It is not an offer of marriage. I can refuse. It came only yesterday and I haven't had a chance to respond yet."

Her mother's eyes narrowed. She turned and placed the letter back on the desktop before turning slowly, her eyes going to her daughter's bewildered ones.

"You think I'm being too hard on you, but you need to think of the children. You have a big responsibility, so don't fall for some overeager suitor who has no feelings for the children. You need to wait. And *six children*?" She made a snorting noise, as if having so many kids was some kind of sin, evidence of bad character.

In reality, a large family wasn't so unusual in the Amish community. Children were a blessing from God. Annie didn't remind her that she had eight of her own children, a fact that her mother had considered an excellent thing prior to Eli's passing.

Instead, Annie just nodded again. "Yes, Mam."

They worked side by side the remainder of the day, cleaning out the last of the bush beans, plucking the prickly cucumber vines. Seeing all the remaining tomatoes, they decided to cook the vegetables separately and make vegetable soup.

Carrots, onion, parsley, celery, potatoes, corn, and green peppers were all cleaned, sliced, chopped, and added to the copper kettle of boiling tomatoes and parsnips. Navy beans and a large beef bone from the butcher shop, salt, pepper, and some dried chives were dropped into the mix, resulting in the most pleasurable aroma from the kettle house door.

The incident with the letter was pushed to the back of Annie's mind as she focused on the work at hand, and with the girls all helping to wash jars, chop vegetables, and of course, to take turns mowing the grass, the day turned out to be so much better than she had expected. Suvilla was a willing, able-bodied worker, which impressed her grandmother deeply, while Ida chattered happily with her innocent lisp, bringing an occasional smile to the narrow face.

Row after row of glass jars containing the bright vegetable soup filled the counter that afternoon. They ate big bowls of it for lunch, with slices of dark wheat bread spread with the pungent yellow butter that had formed by the steady sloshing of the wooden paddles in the glass butter churn. There were no strawberry or raspberry preserves, and there wouldn't be any deep brown apple butter in the fall. Sugar was a luxury, used mostly for preserving, so the only sweetener was the dark molasses or the amber maple syrup, both of which would have to last till spring. But there was the heavy ginger cake, and fresh peaches from the orchard, with plenty of rich, creamy milk, cups of mint tea with a dollop of maple syrup, and more milk.

Her mother sat back, her stern features mellowed from the full stomach, an occasional smile flickering as Ida kept up her lively flow of words.

"Do you have firewood for winter, Annie?" she asked, as she carried plates to the sink to be washed.

"Not yet. I mean, there is some, of course, to cook with, but the winter's supply hasn't been tackled yet," Annie replied, pouring boiling water from the teakettle into the dishpan.

"*Ach*, Annie. Perhaps I'm too harsh. It must not be easy, this going on by yourself. We don't realize how very much we depend on our men for so many things."

Oh mother, you have no idea, Annie groaned inwardly, but she just gave a soft smile.

"But be very careful of marrying that second time."

"I will."

Warmed by her mother's kind words, she told her about her sister's offer to have the family come live near them.

"After everything the church has done to get you back on your feet here?" Her mother asked, incredulous. "Really, Annie. I'm surprised you'd even consider it."

Annie quickly assured her she wasn't really considering it, that she was just telling her how thoughtful Sarah was to suggest it. Inwardly, she wondered why she hadn't seen it that way before. Yes, she'd been quite ungrateful and would repent. She'd write to her sister tomorrow to thank her and decline her offer.

As she watched her mother drive the horse and buggy down the lane that led to the main road, she turned and shook her head sadly. No, there was no way her mother could know this road of solitude, with its unpredictable twists and turns, the desperation when a cow became sick, the anxiety over the unpaid bills, the lurching of her stomach when winter's chill crept through every available crevice around windows and doors, but the damper was turned low to keep the firewood supply from dwindling too fast. The times when they wore coats to sit in the living room, drew their feet up under blankets, the temperature in the house far below what was considered comfortable.

To pay down on the feed bill meant cooked and fried mush for breakfast, tea and saltine crackers soaked in milk when the coffee ran low. It meant dried navy beans boiling on the back of the stove until the smell of them was no longer appetizing, because the beans would fill their stomachs so they could fall asleep. Annie knew what it meant to be hungry and cold, but figured times were hard for everyone, so there was no sense in mewling complaints like a weak kitten. But her mother's words rankled.

Who would fell the trees and chop the wood? Who would shovel the snow and manhandle the milk cans, feed the horses and chickens and pay the bills, clothe the children and put shoes on their feet before they turned red and calloused by the cold? She would, she supposed. With Suvilla and Enos.

And so she put the letter out of sight, out of mind. For a few days she mulled over how to reject his request kindly, but then the busyness of her days and exhaustion of the evenings took over and she realized a week had passed, and then a month, and by then it seemed less rude just to let it go unanswered. Likely he'd started pursuing someone else by then, anyway, she figured.

Daniel Beiler waited and waited, eagerly checking the mailbox, only to be disappointed time after time. When the heat of summer was blown away by the winds of early autumn, the frost covered the low places like a veil of diamonds, and the pumpkins turned huge and orange on the vine, he sat down at his desk and wrote her another.

She read the letter, sighed, stared off into the distance before looking at the calendar. Six days before a year had passed.

Ach, Mam. Would it be so awful if he simply paid me a visit?

It had been a tough day—the three youngest spent the bulk of the morning arguing over a corn husk doll, Suvilla was beginning to develop a disrespectful attitude that Annie didn't understand and didn't have time to address, two of the cows seemed to be sick, and there was still the matter of chopping enough firewood for the quickly approaching winter. Without the time or energy to obsess over what to do with the letter, she made a quick decision. She wrote a letter in her fine hand, with blue ink on a scrap of paper from her black composition book. Yes, he could pay her a visit on the fifteenth of November. She felt bold, strong. She was a grown woman and could make her own decisions. Look at everything else she was handling on her own!

But she spent the night without sleep, stumbled into the cow stable long after Suvilla and Ephraim had started milking, and began to cry into her bucket of milk before stumbling back into the house, saying she had a stomachache. She sat in a kitchen chair staring at the opposite wall until Suvilla came in, glancing at her mother with something far too close to disgust, and then set to work preparing breakfast, waking Annie from her exhausted reverie.

Chapter Four

WHEN HE SHOWED UP AT HER DOOR ON THAT November evening, there was a raw wind driving icy rain against the north side of the house. It dripped off the edge of the roof, sloshed into low places in the yard, banged loose shutters, and created a sea of slick, half-frozen mud.

The knock was slight—so soft, in fact, that she couldn't be sure she had heard it at all—but when she opened the door, he was there, dressed in the heavy black-capped overcoat, the wide-brimmed woolen hat dripping water. She stepped back, told him to come in. He towered above her, all wet wool and formidable height and width. He shook her hand and held it a fraction too long. She lifted her huge green eyes to his kind ones and he was seized by a sense of belonging, a sense of rightness that could only be described as coming home. He felt himself letting go of the immense loneliness that had been his constant companion for too many years.

She had baked molasses cookies and brewed a pot of spearmint tea. She showed him into the kitchen, wishing she'd had time to scrub the floor. They spoke in soft voices so as not to wake the children sleeping upstairs. He was gentle, relaxed, kind—a combination that was in surprising contrast to his physical height and strength. It was hugely attractive. She didn't try to resist the pull of his gentle voice, but instead allowed it to sustain her, carry her along as the evening unfolded.

He had six children, the oldest being twelve years old. Four were in various grades in the elementary school they attended in Leacock Township, and the two youngest, Joel and John, were at home with him and the *maud*.

"Who is your *maud*?" Annie asked.

He sighed, waved a hand in resignation. "Whoever I can get for the week or the month. It's really hard to find a dedicated girl, although a few of them have stayed longer than that. John was only six months old when Sarah died, so he doesn't remember his mother. Joel says he remembers her, but I doubt it."

"It must be hard."

"Probably not harder for me than it is for you."

"That's very kind, but my children have me in the house providing their needs, whereas for you . . ."

Her voice fell away, suddenly quite shy. She hadn't meant to insinuate, to suggest.

His soft laugh put her immediately at ease.

"Look, we may as well be honest. I need a wife, and have not found anyone suitable in three and a half years. Then I followed my horse to your burning barn, and you were overcome by smoke, remember?"

"Yes," she whispered.

"I have not forgotten that day. The barn raising was a huge disappointment . . . I had so hoped to see you. But I couldn't exactly walk to the house and boldly ask the women, so I let it go. Except I couldn't really let it go . . ."

Annie didn't know what to say, so she sat in silence, suddenly feeling awkward.

"Your new barn looks good," he said, bringing the conversation back to a safe topic.

Annie shook her head wryly. The lamplight cast a soft gleam on her thick brown hair, created contours beneath her lovely green eyes.

His heart thudded, thinking how tired she appeared, the drooping of her heavy lids over the gorgeous green eyes. He wanted to smooth the hair away from her forehead, erase the dark circles below her eyes with his kisses.

It had been so long.

"Yes, the church has been more than sufficient. I will never be able to repay, if I live to be a hundred years old. The alms I have given this year would barely pay for one door. No, the hinges on that door."

He nodded, his eyes never leaving her face. "Times are hard," he murmured.

"Do you think things will get worse?" she asked.

"I think the worst is over."

"Really?"

He forced himself to continue the small talk. "It will be slow, the return of people's trust in government and the large banks. We will remain fearful for a good many years. But with our land and the ability to raise crops, we should be all right. The cities are much worse off than we are."

She nodded, suddenly grateful for every jar down cellar, every potato and onion, the covered cabbages and the celery that remained in the garden, banked with good soil and horse manure.

She took a deep breath, then smiled a small, hesitant smile. "Thank you for reminding me I have so much."

He nodded, then let the silence linger for a few moments.

"What was your first husband like?" he asked abruptly.

"Eli? Oh, he was a good husband and father. Good to the children, a good provider. I had nothing to complain about. We had a good marriage, one I have never regretted."

"So you had a bad time dealing with his death?"

"Yes, I did."

"So if you were to marry again, would that second husband always be compared to the perfection in Eli?"

Annie shook her head. "No, no." Should she tell him about his stormy moods, his angry outbursts? She considered it, but then he was speaking again.

"For me it was quite different. Sarah was . . . well, let's just say she was not always stable. She fell when she was a baby, they say. Her relatives said she had a fractured skull but they never took her to a doctor, so she bled in her brain. I think she was afflicted with a mental condition, but since I am not a doctor, I couldn't say for sure. She was extremely happy and noisy one day, and sunk into a deep sadness the next. Having her babies was always a difficult time, but she loved the little ones, so they kept coming. I washed a lot of dishes and clothes, changed diapers and packed lunches for the school children. Sometimes it was tough, but I had to keep going for her sake. Her mother helped out, and her sisters, but most of it fell on me. But you know how we promise to care for each other, in sickness and in health, so I tried to do my best."

His voice trailed off, infinitely weary.

They spoke more freely after that confession. She told him of the times when Eli was demanding, putting his needs ahead of her own, although she felt bad, even now, mentioning something so trivial.

He saw the good in her, the willingness to submit to a loving husband, while she saw the amazing supporter he had been to a wife that might have been afflicted with a disease of the mind.

"Bad nerves," they called it. Many were institutionalized, incarcerated under unthinkable conditions, so he had done all he could to prevent that.

"Her pneumonia? She ran away in an icy storm, hid in a neighbor's shed till the following day, and almost froze to death after a long and tortuous emotional battle she fought after John was born. I blamed myself for years, but finally found peace in the forgiveness of our Savior."

His voice broke.

"The children never knew. They carried on when their mother had the blues, sang with her on the good days. There was harmony in our house as far as anyone could tell. They thought it normal to see Dat doing the washing or the dishes. For that I am grateful."

Annie felt a great empathy, then. She was in awe of this kind and gentle man who had lived with so much pain and disappointment without complaint.

"Why did she run away?"

"She said I didn't love her, which was what she often said when she fell into depression. I did love her, Annie. The best I could."

"I believe you."

"You do?"

"Yes, I do."

Their eyes met and held. Love was exchanged that night with unspoken communication and mutual admiration.

Rain continued its cold lashing against the north side of the house, replenishing the water table below the rich soil, filling the streams and ponds. Dark clouds railed against an inky night sky, hiding the face of the moon and the stars, but inside the widow's house, a soft warm glow of love and understanding began to flourish.

Lonely hearts were fertile ground for the sowing of love, and the night had already turned toward morning when he silently crept out of the house and drove his horse slowly and without the benefit of lantern light until he was safely out of sight.

"Someone was here last night," Suvilla announced at the breakfast table.

Annie had her back turned, making tea at the stove, so she stayed there until she felt the color leave her face. Then she turned slowly but didn't meet their questioning eyes.

"Well?" Suvilla queried again.

Enos shrugged his shoulders. Ephraim said she was dreaming. Ida cut her corn mush and ignored them all.

"It sounded like a man's voice, Mam. You were talking, too."

Suvilla was old enough to know, and to speak her mind, so Annie slowly lifted a finger to her lips, drew down her eyebrows to mimic the "sh." Suvilla's eyes widened, but she closed her mouth and said nothing more.

When they were alone, Annie told her, haltingly.

"What? Who is he? Does he have children?"

Suvilla drew back, staring open mouthed at her mother in disbelief. Annie stumbled over her words, but answered her questions honestly, trying not to show embarrassment. She explained that he was the one who helped her on the day of the fire, that he had six children, that he had requested that they start a friendship.

"*Six* children?"

Annie nodded. Suvilla shot her a look of disbelief, but swallowed any other comments. Children were expected to obey their parents in the Lord. Annie ended the conversation and went about the chores, knowing that if she were apologetic or dragged the discussion on it would only give Suvilla opportunity to voice rebellion. No, it was better to maintain her role as parent—to be loving but firm, not to burden Suvilla with decision-making responsibility beyond her years. It was better for children to have clear boundaries, to follow the Ten Commandments, which included respecting their parents. It gave them a sense of security, even in their teenage years.

After Suvilla found out, she lay awake listening every time Daniel Beiler visited. She resisted the urge to wake Ida, who lay beside her, the cold beginning to creep across the floor and through the uninsulated walls. She couldn't make out most of the words, but she heard the drone of Daniel's voice, the soft answer in her mother's, and imagined how her mother must feel. She was old enough to know the shy glances of young men, to dream of "going steady" someday.

But it was odd to know her own mother was possibly falling in love.

It was toward the end of November when he asked her to marry him. Still, only the oldest children were told, and none of their friends or extended family. The marriage would have to wait till March, as they had to sort through logistics such as the sale of the farm.

Annie walked with a new spring in her step, a new light in her eyes. Daniel was everything to her now. His proposal had been so kind, so gentle, so full of promise. He was concerned about her welfare, the immense responsibility of the combination of their families. "Fourteen kids," he said wryly, and she giggled softly. He took her small capable hand in his and asked her if she was really ready for that kind of challenge.

"With your help, yes. I am."

He would never forget the immensity of those words.

Annie butchered the fattest chicken for Christmas dinner. She made traditional *roasht* with it, roasting the chicken until the meat could easily be pulled off the bones, then mixing it with bread cubes, celery, onion, eggs, salt and pepper. The skin of the chicken was put through the meat grinder, for added richness of flavor. The liver, heart, and gizzard were all ground as well, minced into the other ingredients until it all came together in a savory stuffing dotted with pieces of dark and white chicken, returned to the oven to bake until it was golden brown. There were plenty of potatoes that had been dug in the good, dark earth and then carried carefully into the cellar to be stored in the bin. So Annie peeled and cut a plentiful amount and put them on the back of the cook stove to boil while she used the chicken broth to make gravy. The cabbage had been shredded, mixed with what sugar could be spared, salt, and vinegar, and set in a cool place. There were sliced turnips, lima beans cooked with salt and butter, tiny sweet pickles and dark red beets pickled in a brine with their own juice.

She made two pumpkin pies using molasses and maple syrup for sweetener, and put a sprig of holly on top of each. It wasn't the Amish way to adorn their homes with Christmas trees or wreaths, but the children decided that Christmas that they would take their mam's pies over any fancy English decorations. Each child got one wedge of the smooth, creamy pie, and they savored every bite.

The woodstove crackled and burned, giving the warmth that spread cheer throughout the house. They heaped their plates with the fragrant *roasht* and the mounds of buttery potatoes and thick, rich gravy. Dan had tried to give her money to buy the children gifts, but she had declined, said it wouldn't be proper—especially before they were married. They had never done gifts for Christmas anyway—it wasn't a tradition she had grown up with, her mother having thought gifts distracted from the true meaning of Christmas, the celebration of the Christ child. So there were no gifts on that cozy evening, but the children felt as if it was the best Christmas ever.

Chapter Five

ALL ACROSS LANCASTER COUNTY THE SNOW blew in from the northeast, tiny particles that made a swishing sound as it was driven across metal roofs, hard-packed frozen earth, and ponds. The wind moaned in the pine trees, whistled around the eaves of the house, and threw particles of frozen snow against window panes like sand. The atmosphere was heavy, gray, with a yellowish cast that seemed ominous.

Annie lifted her face to the sky as she made her way to the barn, the driven snow like pellets against it. This was a real January blizzard, and she was prepared, reveled in it. She loved the snow, the purity of winter scenery, when weeds and mud and unsightly puddles were all hidden under the beauty of white, white snow, with blue shadows in hollows and beneath trees that made the whole world seem magical somehow.

And now she was so happy. Her future had changed from the gray of care and responsibility to a wonderful life with a man she loved beyond reason. He was everything she had ever imagined any man could be—kind, caring, soft-spoken, and so pleasant to look at. She loved his eyes, the straight, fine nose, the mouth that curved into a beautiful smile when he arrived in the evenings.

She lifted her arms and gave herself up to the joy that coursed through her veins, skipped a few steps, then reined herself in to a sedate walk. Oh, but it felt wonderful to experience joy again. To feel loved and desired.

Two more months till her wedding day.

It was sobering, thinking of these six children she had never met, but she would love them to the best of her ability. As he would love her own.

The breakfast table held the hum of anticipation as the children looked forward to the snow and all the sledding and sleigh rides. The boiled cornmeal was served with molasses and milk, the bread toasted in the huge cast iron pan on top of the stove. The coffee was steaming hot and so good laced with plenty of cream.

There was firewood in the woodshed, staples in the pantry, enough to keep the hunger away. Annie felt blessed beyond measure, filled with an appreciation for God's kindness, the love he bestowed on them, the richness of life.

On Saturday evening Daniel handed her twenty dollars and told her to buy fabric or shoes, whatever they needed for the wedding.

Annie told him she couldn't take it. "No, no. It's too much. I have a good Sunday dress. It's blue."

She didn't tell him it was eight or nine years old, had been sponged and pressed numerous times, worn thin at the underarms.

"No, Annie. Take it. I want you to have a wedding dress."

She blushed, a gentle rose color that spread like a rose across her cheeks. This time she accepted, not wanting to disappoint him.

They made the decision to move to his farm, as the house was larger and would better accommodate fourteen children. They would add her eight cows to his herd. They would butcher the pigs, add her chickens to the flock.

Annie had never seen the farm, had only a vague idea of where it was located. She would be moving out of her home and the church district she had always known, but that was all right. She would be Mrs. Dan Beiler, mother of fourteen children, able to hold up her head as a woman and mother in the community.

Annie smiled at Daniel, and he smiled back.

They did not touch, only communicated what they felt with their eyes.

They had both been married before. The kisses would wait.

She was taken to his farm to meet the children only a week before the wedding, after the public announcement had been made in church. Now that their secret had been revealed, they would be able to travel together in broad daylight, to be seen in stores or to visit family. Her parents had been told, and though her mother had raised her eyebrows with a mixture of surprise and disapproval, she had kept her tongue quiet as she cleaned the house and made sure she had cabbage and potatoes down cellar for the wedding meal. Annie would butcher her old hens to make the *roasht*.

Daniel's children were shy, peering at her with curious eyes. Amos was a small version of his father with straight dark hair, the wide mouth. Annie took his politely proffered hand, said, "Hello, Amos." Lavina, Hannah, and Emma were like three peas in a pod, all born only a year apart. Dark-haired, dark eyes, curious, their faces were open and honest. Annie gripped their hands and felt a surge of tender love for the motherless trio.

"Hello, hello," she said, smiling warmly.

The three girls responded to Annie's warmth with hungry eyes, wide and lonely and searching. For too long their lives had contained no mother, no solid, unchanging figure they could depend on, no one to cuddle and cherish them, to listen to their little girl woes and joys. There were maids who came and went, washed clothes and dishes and floors, ironed and cooked and baked. Most of them were pleasant, but distant. It was their job to meet the children's tangible needs, but not to love them with the tenderness of a mother.

So when the genuine interest shone from Annie's eyes, they absorbed the warmth of her love and felt rescued. They stood side by side, their eyes never leaving her face. Annie felt reassured that their families would meld easily, that they'd become one just as she and Dan were becoming one.

Joel and John were old enough to know there was tremendous importance in this woman. This was not another *maud*; she was to be their mother. They weren't too sure about someone actually marrying their father and living there, but they remained seated on kitchen chairs, shook hands when it was expected of them, and observed.

"So now you have met your future Mam," Dan said eagerly.

Amos nodded. The three girls responded with hearty smiles and a vibrant yes. Joel and John merely stared, wide-eyed.

"You know she has eight children of her own. You will meet them before the wedding. We will all live together here, so we'll have to make arrangements where everyone will sleep."

Amos shifted from one foot to the other, flicked the straight dark bangs on his forehead.

"Is there someone my age?" he asked timidly.

"Enos is thirteen," Annie said.

Amos smiled. "I'll be his friend."

Annie smiled back, but winced, thinking of Ephraim and Ida's inseparable bond. Would they open up to include Amos? Well, she'd tell them that's what was expected of them, and they would obey. They were good children.

She sewed a new blue wedding dress. Her old black cape and apron would do. The children were equipped with new dresses or trousers as needed, but they did not all have something new to wear.

The farm was sold to Henry Blank for his son Josiah, who would be bringing his new bride in the fall. Annie spent a few hours in tearful nostalgia, then she straightened herself up, realizing a door in her life had been closed and a new one was opening. God had mercy on her existence and was ushering in the beginning of a new life, and she was thankful. She would take this in stride, be a mother to his six children, and never look back.

Her mother was a hard worker, a strict overseer of all the wedding preparations, which was a relief to

Annie. She spent a few days helping with the house-cleaning, but had a huge amount of work herself, preparing for the move to Dan's farm.

The wedding would be held in her parents' large farmhouse, which meant every piece of furniture would be moved into the adjacent woodshed to make room for the setting of wooden benches. And woe to the *hausfrau* who was caught with rolls of dust or spiderwebs beneath bureaus or cabinets, resulting in unmerciful teasing from the men in the family. No, Annie's meticulous mother would never be caught with a job half done. The furniture was cleaned and polished, upended and swept underneath, and the living room rugs were hung over the clothesline and beaten until no dust puffed off of them. The kettles were scoured and polished, for no worthy woman would be caught at wedding time with less than a mirror-like gleam on all the cookware.

The celery was banked with manure-rich soil, the cabbage round and full, but that had been in the fall of the year. By March, what had been harvested in the fall had been consumed out of necessity, celery and cabbage being quick to rot. So her mother made a trip to the greengrocer in Intercourse and handed Dan Beiler the bill with pursed lips and narrowed eyes. Vegetables in March were dear, she told him, standing by while he wrote her a check in his careful hand.

Annie's children, all eight of them, were properly introduced to Dan and his six sons and daughters, a quiet, awkward meeting that all of them were relieved to be done with. It was just so strange, looking at a group of children who would be living in the same house for the rest of their youth.

None of Annie's kids were too sure about Dan. He was large and different, his voice too soft and pillowy for a father. Their real father, the one that died, had been smaller and quicker, his voice loud. If he said something, anything at all, they knew he meant business.

So when this new father was soft-spoken and kind, smiled a lot, and addressed each one individually with gentle words, they weren't quite sure what to make of it.

They were married on a cold, windy day in March, when the sun shone weakly behind scudding clouds and wind bent the trees into perfect C's, whipped bare branches in a frenzy, sent men and women scurrying between house and barn, shawls flapping, men's hands plopped on hat tops.

But inside there was light from gas lights, warmth from the woodstoves, voices, laughter, and an aura of celebration. The house was filled to capacity with voices rising in plainsong, the slow rise and fall of old German hymns from the heavy black *Ausbund*. They were pronounced man and wife by his uncle, Stephen Beiler, from over toward Leola, a bishop who was well known for his fiery sermons.

The fourteen children sat on benches with varying degrees of attentiveness, but all had the same bewildered expression, a vacant wondering of the future created by the joining of the two people who sat side by side in the minster's row, looking as if this was the most serious moment of their lives.

But later they all enjoyed the festivities, the plates of good, hot chicken filling, mashed potatoes, and gravy. There was plenty of cake, pie, doughnuts, and cookies, with cornstarch pudding and grape mush. The children sat in a respectful row, ate with gusto, and tried not to think too much about how different their lives were about to be.

And so life began for Dan and Annie Beiler in 1932, on the farm he inherited from his parents on Hollander Road. He had inherited money from them as well, and had managed it well so that it had grown, despite the Depression. The house was substantial. Built of gray limestone, the mortar was as thick as seaworthy rope and the walls were so thick the windowsills easily held a variety of potted plants. There were six bedrooms upstairs, with a staircase along the front of the house and one in the back. The wealthy landowners who designed and built the house at the turn of the century, in 1798, had built the narrow curved staircase in the back for the servants' use.

The kitchen ran along the side of the house that faced the large stone barn, with cabinets built by a German Baptist named Wesley Overland, well known for his distinctive style. There were polished hardwood floors and rugs scattered throughout the house tastefully. The furniture was far better than anything Annie had ever owned, so she appreciated the cherry sleigh beds and the heavy ornate dressers and bureaus. There were plenty of bed linens, patchwork quilts and heavy comforters made with sheep's wool. They stretched the long kitchen table to add even more leaves to accommodate the eight children and their mother. There was an indoor bathroom with a porcelain commode, but no bathtubs—at that time they were frowned on in Amish homes and pronounced an unnecessary worldly luxury.

Annie could hardly believe this magnificent dwelling was now hers. She had never imagined an indoor facility to use the restroom, and certainly not in an Amish home. She realized Dan was a bit of a progressive, living in such comfort, plus the way he was outspoken about other modern inventions.

She cleaned and scoured, made up freshly washed beds with sheets and pillowcases just off the line. Dan told her to paint rooms wherever she felt a need, but she was appalled at the thought of spending money only to change the appearance of a room if it was perfectly serviceable without. She washed the walls, though, with a bucket of soapy water and a heavy cloth, wiping and scrubbing till her shoulders ached with fatigue.

When she was finished, she took stock of her situation and thought it quite manageable, really. Suvilla slept with Ida in a big double bed in the front room toward the barn. Lavina, Emma, and Hannah slept in the other front room, across the hallway.

Annie allowed Dan's girls to stay in one room, and her own girls to stay in another. They had enough to merely become acquainted without having to share a bed. She put Amos with Joel and John, who all fit together in one bed nicely enough. She thought twelve-year-old Amos might appreciate being responsible for his smaller brothers.

Sammy was reserved a small room in the back, the former servant's quarters, with only a single bed and dresser. He was more than pleased with this arrangement, having easy access to his own staircase to sneak in and out of the house whenever a bit of mischief beckoned.

Enos and Ephraim were tremendously happy to be allowed a room of their own without having to host Amos. Amos the Intruder, as they called him when they were alone. They knew it was wrong to think of him in those terms, but that's what he was. He was always trying to get in on their private jokes or games, and it was a hassle to have to stop and try to explain everything.

The oblong room was left for the other Emma, Lydia, and Rebecca, the three little girls who were delighted to sleep in a sizable room together. There were two beds with a small stand in between, a place to put handkerchiefs and water glasses.

So that left one small room in the back for guests. Every respectable Amish home needed a comfortable guest room for overnight visitors, folks who traveled twenty or thirty miles with a horse-drawn carriage and needed a place to stay before they could make the return trip. To cook a delicious meal, to stable and feed the weary horse, was an honor. Most Amish families looked forward to receiving visitors. The parents would share stories and news over the dinner table as the children eyed one another with shy glances and listened with intrigue. Plus, company was a good excuse to bring out the sack of white sugar and bake a golden pound cake with brown sugar frosting.

Of course they would be getting visitors after their
marriage, so Annie whipped everything into order
in a few weeks' time, just in time to drop seeds into
the well-worked soil. The garden had been plowed
to double its size, with nine more hungry mouths
to feed. The flower beds were dug with fresh cow
manure, the lawnmower sharpened and oiled, before
the lawn was neatly mowed and trimmed.

The bedroom downstairs contained the furniture
Annie had brought, with one of her quilts made up
neatly on the high, iron bed frame. There was a rather
large sampler on the wall, done in cross stitched
embroidery, with the words "East or West, Home is
Best" done in heavy black lettering with a design of
roses in a myriad of brilliant colors. The frame was
made of natural wood by Eli's own hand, so Annie
cherished this bit of frivolity more than anything she
had brought.

Dan was gentle, caring, all she could ever want or
need. To lie in his arms with the shrill cheeping of
the spring peepers down at the pond, the breeze from
the soft spring night like a balm from paradise, knowing she was loved, cherished, and so very appreciated

was the closest thing to Heaven. But in the morning, there were challenges in the form of six children who were expected to accept the eight of her own into their home and lives. They sat in out-of-the-way corners and glowered when she became happy or silly with one of her own. She tried her best to draw Amos into a lively morning discussion, but he retaliated by his sullen look before letting himself quickly out the door. If Enos or Ephraim—at Annie's prompting—tried to win him over, he thwarted all attempts at companionship with handfuls of thrown dirt and hurled swear words.

As problems arose, they dealt with them, although Annie had days when she wondered why she had ever thought another marriage was God's will for her life. Especially days when the two Emmas locked horns, fighting and arguing and then pouting, disobeying her orders simply because they felt so miserable inside. "Emma One" and "Emma Two," they called them. Neither one thought it was amusing. Each Emma wanted her own identity, and certainly did not want to share with the other.

Chapter Six

THEY HAD EGGS FOR BREAKFAST NOW. GOOD brown eggs with dark orange yolks and glossy whites fried perfectly in hot lard and salted and peppered to perfection. They should have been sold and the money gone toward other household expenses, Annie reasoned.

"Now why would we do that?" Dan asked, patting her shoulder affectionately.

"Eggs are a good profit," she answered.

"You can't eat profit," he laughed. "I love a good fried egg in the spring, and why should I eat eggs and the children go without? I say we should eat them as long as the hens are laying."

Enos and Ephraim nodded, their eyes never leaving their stepfather's face. All of Annie's children lived with Dan, looked to him as a hero of deliverance. There were eggs for breakfast, more meat, even if it was merely slivers of beef in white milk gravy. There were pies, and occasionally cookies made with molasses, white flour, and sugar. Instead of bread with lard they had soft white bread and butter, sometimes with pear or apple butter.

But Dan's children looked on the eight Miller children as usurpers, upending their own stable relationship with their remaining parent, and used every available opportunity to remind them of this.

Walking home from school was the worst time, when they were safely out of earshot of both parents.

"Emma, get off the road. There's a car coming," Amos shouted.

Emma One, his biological sister, called back, "Which Emma?" Although both Emmas stepped closer to the ditch, out of the way of the oncoming vehicle.

"You! There is no other Emma who is my sister."

Wide-eyed, seven-year-old Emma's feelings were extremely hurt. Tears formed as she hastily stuck her thumb in her mouth.

"She is too your sister," Ephraim shouted.

"No, she's not."

"Is too."

"Huh-uh."

Lunch boxes were thrown in the ditch, fists balled, and heads lowered as they met head on by the side of the road, hitting and pounding.

"Get offa me!" Amos yelled.

"Say she's your sister and I will," Ephraim grunted, pounding away while he straddled his back.

With both hands over his ears, Amos kept shouting. "She's not my real sister!"

Enos entered into the fray, always the peacemaker, trying to pull Ephraim off by his suspenders. Ida, always the tomboy, egged Ephraim on, saying, "Get him! Make him say 'Uncle!'"

Bloodied and mud-stained, the two boys crept up the back stairway, changed clothes, and wiped their faces as best they could, but neither one could hide the black eye or the raw scratches and bruises.

They sat on the bench to change socks, as guilty as thieves. Annie turned, already aware of unusual goings on, the way those two had crept up the back stairs. She laid down the towel she was folding and walked over to where they were seated.

Why was it so much easier to reprimand Ephraim than Amos? She so desperately wanted to feel the same about both boys, and yet there was a difference. She felt afraid, intimidated by Amos.

Ephraim had been hers since the day he was born. She had fed and diapered him, watched him take his first step, and he was a part of her life, a part of her being. Amos was acquired at the age of thirteen, and had not been hers at all one moment before then. She had to remind herself repeatedly that he was indeed hers, that he became hers the day she married Dan.

"What happened?" she began.

"Ephraim beat me up," Amos offered, sullenly, without remorse.

"What do you have to say for yourself?" she asked quietly.

"Mam, he said our Emma was not his sister, and she is, too."

"So that gave you enough reason to beat him?" Annie asked.

"He made her cry."

Why was it so hard to tear her eyes away from Ephraim's face and into Amos's? She felt so badly for both boys, but knew she needed to be courageous, to face this situation squarely.

Taking a deep breath, she plunged in.

"Alright, both of you."

She met the glowering eyes of her stepson.

"The day we were married, we became a family, alright? In God's eyes, we have fourteen children, so it's up to you to accept this. Emma is your sister, Amos. Yes, she is. She was not born your sister, but through marriage, she is. So we will hear no more of this about who is whose sister or brother."

Both boys were shame-faced now, felt their mistake by the spare words of a strong mother. And yet they felt her caring heart, too, even if they wouldn't have admitted it in that moment.

"We are all family. We aren't perfect, but no family is. Amos, you had no right to say Emma was not your sister. We won't say things like that again, OK?"

He nodded, his eyes downcast.

"Ephraim, apologize for beating him. Amos, apologize for saying that."

Ephraim spoke up.

"He shouldn't apologize to me. He should tell Emma he's sorry. I was sticking up for her."

"That can come later. Right now this is about you two."

They offered halfhearted apologies, but there was no real feeling. Annie decided it was enough that they had obeyed and left it at that, ushering them out to do chores.

When suppertime came, she had all the wash folded, and with Suvilla's help, it was all put back in drawers and closets, except for a stack of ironing in the clothesbasket. She was stirring the thick bean soup, her back turned to the kitchen, when she felt two strong hands grasp her waist, followed by Dan's face close to hers and a soft kiss placed on her cheek.

"My *glaeyne frau*," he murmured.

She smiled, leaned back against his chest for a moment. He smelled of wet earth and strong breezes, of cows and hay and, yes, manure. The smell she had been used to all her life. The smell of a farmer.

She turned to meet his eyes, the tender look she found there as sure as the rising sun. His temperament never changed. He was like a rock, a pillar of good humor and gentleness that supported the foundation of her being. When she was with him, nothing seemed impossible.

"I love you," she whispered, a hand going to his face. He smiled into her eyes, and they both turned to find many pairs of eyes watching them.

Dan smiled, stepped back, clapped his hand and said, "*Komm*, Rebecca." He beckoned her two-year-old. *Our two-year-old*, she reminded herself. *Not just mine*.

"*Komm*," he coaxed again. Rebecca watched him warily, then sidled shyly along the sofa until she reached him. He bent to pick her up, cradled her in his lap while she put her thumb in her mouth and closed her eyes.

They all laughed.

Rebecca was so shy, and her thumb was her refuge from every scary thing in her life. Closing her eyes was her way of shutting out whatever her thumb did not console.

"Funny girl, Rebecca," Dan laughed, holding her closer.

As Annie dished up the fragrant bean soup, a stab of guilt went through her, took away the comfort of

Dan's attentiveness. It all seemed so easy for him, so seamless. There was no effort in his reaching for her child; the attempts to win her over were completely genuine. Already the younger girls adored him, especially Lydia and Emma. For this, Annie was thankful, but it highlighted her own shortcomings.

The dinner table held two loaves of bread, three large dishes of apple butter, three plates of butter, and the steaming bowls of bean soup. There were fourteen hungry children lined on either side of the lengthy table. Dan sat at the end of the table, with Annie to his left, Rebecca on her other side.

The chattering and scraping of chairs stopped the minute Dan lifted a hand. "*Patties noona.*" It was the signal to bow heads in unison, hands in laps, as silent prayers were whispered or thought, depending on the person's method of thanking the Lord for the food before them. Some children were conscientious, lowering their heads so their foreheads almost touched the tabletop, while others bowed their heads only slightly, their eyes sliding sideways while their elbows poked into ribs, snickers or whispers escaping them.

Ephraim didn't bow his head at all, resulting in a
stern look from Dan.

Ephraim said he didn't know how Dan could see
what he was doing if he kept his own head bowed the
way he was supposed to. Amos countered that every
parent was expected to watch his children's behavior;
it didn't matter when. Enos rolled his eyes, knowing Amos would side with Dan (he could not bring
himself to call him "Dat"), regardless of his actions.

They did get visitors. They descended on the Dan
Beiler farm like a swarm of flies, trickling in one at a
time, till there were as many as six or seven buggies
parked along the front of the barn, or tied to the
hitching rack, on any given Sunday.

They came to welcome Annie and her children.
They wrung her hand, clasped it in both of their
own, looking deep into her eyes with much love
and understanding. They brought doughnuts and
apple dumplings, sacks of licorice and pans of
scrapple.

Ezra Lapp sie Anna handed her a bag of fresh lettuce and new red radishes, perfect red globes tied in

a neat bundle with a rubber band secured around the green tops.

"Already?" Annie gasped, throwing her hands in the air.

"My now, Annie. Don't you have a hot bed?"

Annie shook her head no.

"*Mold oh*. We need to talk to Dan. Can hardly believe he didn't build a hot bed for Sarah. Any worthy frau needs a hot bed to sow lettuce and radish seeds in February or early March." With that, she took herself into the living room to shake Dan's hand and accost his unworthiness by not having a hot bed.

Dan looked into her face as she talked, nodded his head up and down in affirmation, said ya, ya, he would have to see to it. Then he did the unthinkable and told her he already had a warm bed with his new wife and that was *far* more important, which caused her to blush and snort and pshaw her way back to the kitchen as fast as possible.

Ezra Lapp was not a farmer. He started a welding shop in the twenties, called K and L Welding, and made a fairly good living for the first five years, till the Depression took away most of his trade. A quiet, unassuming man, he was married to an out-spoken robust woman four years his senior, who seemed to control him much the same way a puppet is controlled, by deft manipulation. Everyone knew when shy Ezra asked for her hand in marriage she told him she would marry him on one condition, and that was that he not milk cows or farm the land, that she was not going to smell cow manure and sour milk her whole life long. Some said he should have been warned by that; others said he wasn't dumb, he enjoyed his garrulous, decisive wife.

They said she was the one who had the funds to start up K and L Welding, that the K stood for her maiden name, Kauffman. He seemed perfectly happy to be put in the back seat and let his outspoken wife do most of the talking. He listened to her spit-flinging tirades with acceptance and interest, for he loved his round wife and admired her mind immensely. But when Dan told her about his warm bed, he threw back his head and howled with glee. He had never seen his Anna quite as flummoxed as he had then, and was delighted.

Back in the kitchen with Annie, Davey Zook sie Katie said a good way to stretch meat was to put it in *roasht*, that any meat was good that way, even ground beef or sausage. In fact, her favorite was *doggie fils*, which was *roasht* made with sliced hot dogs. She looked hopefully in Annie's direction, wondering if she would be the kind of wife to welcome others to her table. She was not disappointed when Annie said, "We could have it for supper. Will you all be staying?"

"Yes. Oh, indeed. Sure. But don't go to any bother, please."

The women rose as one to help peel potatoes and cut bread into cubes. There was no celery in spring, so they used onion and dried parsley, plenty of lard, and cut up canned hot dogs, and mixed everything in an enormous bowl with beaten eggs and chicken broth. Then they dumped it into a large roaster and popped it in the wood-fired oven.

Potatoes were put on the range to boil, milk gravy made with browned butter and flour, canned beans seasoned with salt, pepper, molasses, and a bit of pork fat. The meal was rounded out with bowls of applesauce, small dishes of sweet pickles, and pickled red beets.

The men and children ate first, which allowed the women to serve them, the traditional way of hosting a Sunday table for visitors. There were twenty-three present at the extended table, and all ate with a hearty appetite, even the smallest boy or girl.

Katie watched the men taking second helpings of the *doggie fils* onto their plates. She so loved it, and hadn't made it in a while, so her mouth watered all through. "The men always take so long," she told the other women in the kitchen.

"Oh, but they're hungry," Annie answered from her point at the stove, dishing up the fragrant beans.

"Well, we are, too. *Ach*. Annie, you're too sweet for your own good. *Hesslich*, everyone is going to walk all over you."

"Oh no," Annie laughed. "I can speak my mind. But after you have been a widow for a while, things look so much different. Appreciation comes more easily."

They saw the tears in her eyes, and everyone was touched. Here was a woman who had suffered bravely, who had carried on in these hard times, and didn't seem to hold the slightest bitterness in her heart.

Annie served bread and butter, along with strawberry preserves. Dessert was her high, quivering custard pie, a real treat for those who seldom had extra eggs or milk. There were clear glass bowls of canned peaches and a dense spice cake thick with raisins, nutmeg, and cinnamon.

Oh, it was a wondrous meal, especially for Depression times.

Dan himself had no idea the custard pies had been made on Saturday morning, along with the twice weekly ten loaves of bread. The spice cake smell had lingered in the kitchen at lunchtime, but he'd figured it was a bread pudding for supper.

The women all asked for the custard pie recipe, and the men thought Dan a very fortunate man, even before the appearance of spice cake and peaches.

"You have a good cook, Dan," Henry Beiler said, leaning back in his chair and patting his full stomach with appreciation.

Annie's face was flushed, moving from table to stove, filling bowls and water glasses, replenishing the bread plate.

Eventually, Dan looked around the table to be certain he was not hurrying a slow eater, before he spoke. "Did you get enough?"

Murmurs of appreciation and assent followed.

Dan smiled, cleared his throat, and ducked his head to thank the Lord for what they had just eaten in the second silent prayer.

Whooping with glee, the children and their friends slid off benches and made a mad dash for the door to continue their game of kickball. The men chewed on toothpicks or smoked their pipes or cigars in the living room. The women hurriedly cleared the table, emptied serving bowls into heavy kettles, and reheated, stirred, and reset the table, talking, laughing, enjoying the camaraderie. Sunday company was the high point of many hardworking women's social lives.

The table was almost filled the second time, and there was enough for everyone. Not everyone got a slice of the spice cake, but there was plenty of pie and peaches. The women all said they didn't know when they ever had better *doggie fils*. Annie demurred, saying it wasn't better than anyone else's, although she did add more chicken broth and eggs than her mother used to.

The house was messy, the floors tracked with muddy foot prints, and all the work she had put into the preparing of pies and cakes had disappeared in one Sunday evening. But the time of making new friends, the enjoyment of hospitality and fellowship, far outweighed the work.

By the time all the kids were in bed or in their rooms and Annie and Dan finally got to turn in for the night, her body ached with weariness. But her heart was filled with gratitude. She kissed her new husband, lay her head on his strong arm, and thanked him for everything he did for her. They both fell asleep with a smile on their lips.

Chapter Seven

As spring turned into summer, Annie's workload doubled, at least. The sun's rays increased, drawing the many seeds into sprouts, the sprouts into beanstalks, potato plants, pea vines, and more. She stood to survey the sheer size of her garden.

It was a dewy morning, after a few days of intermittent rain and drizzle, so the weeds had gathered in force, taking over the well-tilled and hoed soil until it looked like a sea of green. And it was wet. So wet. How would they ever restore the garden to its original manicured state? She would be ashamed to have the neighbors see this. But then she smiled to herself, remembering that everyone's garden had been rained on, not just hers.

And it was a lovely morning. The dew was like jewels scattered across the yard, the lush green plants beaded with them, dripping off the perfect green leaves. The sun was a fiery ball of orange, already pulsating with the heat that left men leaning against a fence post, their hats tilted back as they swiped at rivulets of perspiration.

This was the time of homemade root beer, mint tea, and ginger water taken to the hayfields where the men forked loads of loose hay onto a wooden wagon drawn by faithful mules or Belgians. This was when every single vegetable from the garden was eaten or canned to put down cellar for the coming winter. For the hundredth time, Annie was grateful to have a kind and gentle husband, and the anxiety of providing for her family alone taken from her shoulders. She loved his strength, his way with the children, his patience and gentleness. How could it be that God had blessed her when she most certainly did not deserve all this?

She turned and went back into the house, only to find Joel and John, five and four, who were Dan's youngest children, in a heated argument with five-year-old Lydia, who was her own.

Oh, she hated that she still thought of them as *her* children and *his* children, but how else was she to make sense of the constant bickering and rivalry? These children had gone through so much, losing their mother and father, struggling with grief and childish sorrow, before being thrown together to live in one house. Remembering this gave her the compassion she needed to deal with the daily struggle of peacekeeping and discipline.

Joel was nearly six now, dark haired and dark eyed, with a brilliant mind and the vocal cords of a little preacher. He ruled John, who was a gentle, passive child, happy to go along with whatever his older brother wanted. Five-year-old Lydia, on the other hand, had inherited all the spit and vigor of Annie's own mother, including the loud voice and quick temper.

Joel and Lydia had both woken up in a foul mood, the heat upstairs causing them to sleep fitfully. Thirsty, unable to find their mother, they sat on the old davenport like uncomfortable little birds, eyeing each other, with sweet-natured John between them.

"Where's Mam?" John asked, his strident voice like a razor to Lydia's ill temper.

"She's not your mother."

"Yes, she is. She's as much our mam as she is your mam," Joel answered.

"How do you figure that?" Lydia sat forward, slid her feet to the floor, and twisted her head toward him, suspicion and challenge in her eyes.

"Well, you know. Since the wedding. We're all your mam's kids, and my dat is your father, too."

"Don't say 'kids.' Only English people say 'kids.'"

"Kids, kids, *kids*!" Joel said loudly.

"Stop it. Stop it this minute."

"Kids."

With her hand on her hips, Lydia faced her opponent squarely. "You say that one more time, and I'm going to the barn and telling Dat."

"No! No!"

Now that Lydia had the upper hand, she wasted no time in using her power to its full advantage, taunting him with every misdeed of the day before, of which there were plenty.

They both began to yell, which was how Annie found them when she entered the kitchen.

Again, it was easiest to tackle her own Lydia, before turning to the irate Joel, and by now, the deeply troubled John.

"What happened? Stop this now, both of you."

Lydia was indignant, her face flushed with anger. "He said we were 'kids.' Only goats have kids, and we are not supposed to say that."

"No, we don't say that, Joel. You are '*kinna*.'" Annie answered calmly.

"He just kept saying it," Lydia pouted, crossing her arms around her waist.

"I did not!"

"Yes, you did. Mam, he's telling a *schnitza*. He always lies!"

"Lydia, you go sit on that chair." Annie pointed to a cane-bottomed chair in the corner. "Even if you're right, you're being prideful and unkind." She turned to Joel. "What started this?"

Sullen, he refused to meet her eyes. She waited.

Finally, he spoke. "She said you were not my mother, and I said you were. At the wedding, the preacher said we all became one."

Annie's stern face softened. She could see the hurt and confusion beneath his petulant scowl.

"Yes, Joel, we are. We are all one family. We all live together in this big stone house and we all have to try and get along. I am everyone's mother, and

Dat is everyone's father." She turned to Lydia. "So, Lydia, it wasn't right to say what you said. And Joel, never refer to any of your brothers or sisters as 'kids,' alright?"

He stared at his toes, would not give her the satisfaction of a decent answer. Annie sat beside him, slid an arm around the stone-faced boy, and pulled him close. "Promise me?"

She was shocked when he flung himself into her lap and cried as if his heart would break, which set John into little sputters and then full-fledged howling, too.

Annie's heart seemed to melt within her. She reached out to include John in the hug, squeezing them tight to her as tears sprang to her own eyes.

"It's alright," she murmured, over and over.

She beckoned to Lydia to join their huddle, but she shook her head stubbornly, folding her arms across her chest and watching the display with bitterness glistening in her eyes.

Was ever anything all right, she wondered. She had pronounced these words over and over since the day she married her beloved Dan, but most days there was much more wrong than right. No one could prepare another person for this. It was like walking blindly down a sunlit path, never imagining the obstacles you would meet. Most stepmothers had only a few children, and she'd heard it could be hard, but this?

She thought of her mother's warning against marrying a man who didn't feel for her children. But Dan was fine with the children—he always seemed to know just what to say or how to act around them. Annie, on the other hand, constantly doubted that she was saying or doing the right thing. And there was simply not enough of her to go around. Some days she thought the sting of grief and poverty was easier to handle than the feeling of constant failure and inadequacy.

Suddenly, she could hear her grandmother's voice in her mind. "Annie, can you get nothing right? Must you ruin everything you touch? *Ach*, your poor husband someday. What a mess, Annie. What a mess you are . . ."

Annie felt her stomach clench up, the way it always did when she remembered her grandmother.

She took a deep breath and brought herself back to the present, back to the two needy children beside her. She held the two boys, told them they were very special to her, and that she would always be their real mother.

When Joel sat up and dug out his small, wrinkled handkerchief and wiped his eyes and nose, a shudder passed through him.

He looked up at Annie.

"Do you really mean that? You will always be right here?"

"Oh, I will. I love it here. I love your father and I love you."

The two pairs of eyes turned to her were guileless, the innocent eyes of children who were hungry for love, hungry for assurance of a mother who would never leave them.

From the corner came Lydia's disgusted voice.

"Well, it's nice you like *some* of us, at least."

"Come, Lydia. You know I have always loved you." Then she smiled and said teasingly, "*And* I like you, even when you're kind of a bossy little tattle tale."

At that, Lydia couldn't help but giggle a little, which got the rest of them laughing until their sides hurt.

Breakfast was two loaves of bread sliced and spread with peanut butter, laid in a wide soup plate with sugared coffee that was thick with cream poured over it. They all ate heartily of the good coffee soup, a staple in warm weather when the kitchen range would have to be fired too high to fry all that corn-meal mush. Sometimes Annie made oatmeal and they ate it with apple butter and biscuits, or a huge cast iron pan of fried potatoes, but only on mornings that were cool.

The happy chatter and clatter of spoons on granite plates reminded Annie how easily children forgave each other and moved on with their lives as if nothing had occurred. Dan praised the coffee soup, said the peanut butter really got a fellow going on these hot days. She smiled into his eyes and was rewarded with the tenderest look from his gentle countenance. For the hundredth time, she thought nothing could be impossible with Dan by her side.

Ida and Hannah, both eleven years old, were chosen to do dishes, while Ephraim, Lavina, and Emma were told to help their mother in the garden. Amos and Enos were expected to drive the horses, one to cultivate the cornfield, one to drive the wagon while Dan forked hay.

Suvilla was expected to start the washing. The water was already steaming in the iron kettle. Ida said she didn't know why she couldn't drive the horses. Hannah agreed, saying girls should be allowed to drive. In fact, she'd seen Emery Glick's girls, Fronie and Sadie, drive the hay wagon just the day before. Amos narrowed his eyes and said girls washed dishes and boys drove wagons around. Ida's eyes flashed fire as she sized up her stepbrother, but she kept quiet. Annie breathed easier when Hannah did the same.

Dan listened, smiled, then said probably girls were every bit as good at driving horses as boys, so if they washed the dishes real good for breakfast and dinner, he'd let them try this afternoon, seeing how he needed Amos and Enos to help him fork hay.

The girls looked on their father with an expression close to worship. Annie thanked him with her sweet smile.

Everyone was expected to work hard, right down to the two little Emmas and Hannah. They worked together as a team as the sun rose high over the gardens. The children were all suntanned, their muscles well developed, toughened by physical labor as well as vigorous play. They all knew the work came first, which could last most of the day. The smallest ones carried wooden bushel baskets by the wire handles and gathered the piles of weeds as the older children dug them out with hoes. Sometimes they sang or whistled, calling back and forth across the rows.

It was Hannah who found the first potato bugs. She alerted Ida, who knew exactly what to do, but she figured she'd better talk to her mother first. Annie and Suvilla were in the cellar, sweeping cobwebs and washing shelves that looked quite empty now. They would scour every inch before mixing powdered lime with water, then brushing it over the stone walls of the house's foundation, creating a sparkling white disinfected area to store the summer's bounty.

"Mam!"

"Yes?"

"Potato bugs! Millions of potato bugs!"

"*Ach* my. Wait, I'll help you get kerosene."

She found an old tin can, put on the shelf in the woodshed for this purpose, and poured some of the smelly fuel into it, then selected a short stick and handed it to her.

"There you go, Ida. Be careful to check the undersides of the leaves."

Ida loved this chore, as did the other children.

"Potato bugs!"

"Let me! Let me!"

Everyone swarmed around Ida, eager for a turn at knocking the shiny purplish brown beetles into the kerosene can until they died, which was not long at all. But Ida pushed her way through to the potato plants and began to whack them quite efficiently into their oily demise, with many pairs of keen eyes observing every move she made.

"They're dying," Joel announced solemnly.

"They are supposed to do that," Lydia told him, her nose in the air, taut with her own superiority.

"I know," Joel said.

Lydia, never able to let something go without having the last word, announced triumphantly, "You didn't know till I told you."

"I did. Kerosene kills anything."

"Not everything."

"Almost."

John sat between two rows of beans, snapping a yellow wax bean before putting it in his mouth, his head turning first to Lydia, then to Joel as the exchange continued.

"It doesn't matter," he said loudly.

"What?"

"About kerosene."

"What about it?"

"I don't know."

"I don't either."

Solemnly, the children continued picking up weeds, dragging the heavy wooden bushel basket between them. They did their job well, never complaining, only occasionally stopping for a drink of water. Now and then a conversation broke out, but the work always progressed steadily throughout the forenoon.

At twelve o'clock, Annie washed her hands at the pump, laid out bread and butter and glasses of mint tea for a quick lunch. Dan had gone to help a neighbor with the birthing of a first-time heifer, so there was only a snack. The biggest meal of the day would be after the evening milking.

The afternoon wore on, with the children losing energy as the heat of the sun became almost unbearable. Ida had long ago found the last potato bug, so it was back to hoeing, which did not seem fair at all, the way the weeds were so thick it didn't matter how hard she brought the hoe down, there were more weeds. The hotter it became, the more her temper flared.

"Dat said we could fork hay or drive horses. Instead we're still stuck in this garden," she fumed.

Suvilla was thinning corn, her hair blowing out and away from the kerchief around her head, her face almost the same color as the early cherry tomatoes. She slanted the irritable Ida a look. "What did you expect? Fathers never keep their promises." She pushed her hair back, leaving streaks of sweat and dirt on her forehead. "I, for one, am never getting married."

Ida stopped hoeing and drew down her eyebrows as she mulled over her sister's words. Puzzled, she asked what she meant by that.

"Dat always promised me he'd take care of us, but he didn't," Suvilla said sullenly, just loud enough for Ida to hear.

"But he couldn't help it that he died. He was in an accident."

"He still died."

"So?"

"So I'll never get married."

Ida considered this. "It's not like most husbands die so early," she ventured softly.

"Some do."

"But we have a new Dat, Suvilla. This one is much nicer. We have more to eat, and a bigger, better house. This Dat doesn't raise his voice, or become angry or anything."

"Not yet. He might, though."

Ida leaned on her hoe, looking for all the world like a wise old woman with her head cocked to one side, nodding to herself.

"You know, it's probably a good idea for you to stay

single. If you did get married, your husband would have to live with you constantly worrying about him dying or getting mad. You'd both be miserable."

"What do you know about marriage, Ida?" Suvilla barked.

"Enough to know you better stop feeling sorry for yourself unless you really do want to be a lonely old maid."

There was a loud call from the barn.

"Suvilla, Ida, Hannah! *Kommet!*"

Ida took off in long-legged strides toward the barn, Hannah and the two Emmas toddling behind.

Suvilla's brows lowered, her mouth set in a grim line, and she turned away. Slowly she gathered up the hoes and the bushel baskets, stacked everything in the woodshed, threw the weeds across the fence to the horses, and went to find her mother, who was just finishing up the whitewashing.

Annie took one look at Suvilla's glowering face before setting down the galvanized bucket, placing one hand on a hip, and saying, "What?"

Suvilla brushed past and went into the house, slamming the screen door behind her.

Chapter Eight

THERE WERE TIMES THAT SUMMER THAT Annie was so weary, so bone tired, she felt as if every muscle was protesting against one more step. Yes, it was the physical labor, but more than that it was the constant bickering, the competition between the children for her attention and love, that wore her out. No matter how she tried, she couldn't convince them that there was enough love to go around. Sometimes she thought maybe there *wasn't* actually enough love in her heart. When she lost her patience and snapped at one of the children, or struggled to feel the same way about Dan's little ones as she did about hers, she shuddered to think maybe she was as coldhearted as her unfeeling grandmother.

Every night she set the large round tub on the back porch for the children to wash their feet before bed. Such a long row of sun-browned and calloused feet that had dashed across grass and stones and plowed soil. She helped the little ones scrub and tried to remember to give each child a word of attention, something to let them know she was here, she was their mother, and she loved them all the same.

She tried, but had to admit, there was a difference, in spite of her best efforts. Lavina and Hannah had taken to eyeing her with dark baleful glances, which she ignored at first, but then catalogued as another form of rebellion. She knew she was not enough. There simply was not time to draw out each child and give them the attention—that delicate balance of loving care and discipline—that they needed.

After all the children were upstairs in bed, Annie and Dan retreated to the swing on the front porch. They rocked gently and the swing creaked and groaned from the rusty hooks in the ceiling. Crickets chirped lazily from their hiding place beneath the boxwoods; a procrastinating robin chirped loudly to its mate from the maple branch above them. A cow lowed softly, the sound of her hooves in the barnyard like suction cups, the mud drawing down on each heavy split hoof.

"Barnyard still wet?" Annie asked softly.

"Yes. Guess I'll have to clean it up. We are just blessed with plenty of rain this summer."

Annie laid her head on Dan's solid shoulder and placed a hand on his knee, something she would never have done with her first husband. He had so often carried resentment like a prickly armor, a porcupine of separation. Dan was, well, he was welcoming. His wide chest and shoulders were a haven for her weariness and concerns at the end of the day.

Now, when his arms went around her, drawing her against him, he bent to place a kiss on the top of her head.

"My precious little wife," he said, chuckling in the depth of his chest.

Annie closed her eyes and rested in his love.

"Dan, I'm sorry to come to you every evening with my concerns, but do you think Lavina and Hannah have a . . . have a problem with me?"

For a long moment Dan was quiet, the rise and fall of his chest the only sound. He sighed, cleared his throat, then drew a hand from her waist to her shoulder, where he began a gentle massage.

"Annie my love, I would never hurt your feelings if I could help it, you know that. But I think those two girls were hit very hard by the death of their mother. It wasn't just her passing. They spent a lot of time with her when she was struggling. So to grow up with a . . . a loss of love and attention, then to have to see their mother's passing . . . I always imagine them like leaking little boats pushed out to sea. It's hard for them. And . . . ."

He paused, drew a deep breath.

"I think maybe Ida is causing some jealousy. What do you think?"

Annie held very still. Ida. The one whose boundless energy and high spirits had often carried her through her darkest hours. She was blessed with a sunny disposition and a never-ending flow of good humor, finding ways of fun and delight where many children would have overlooked it. She loved Ida fiercely. It came so naturally. She had always hoped never to favor one above the other, but no one would disagree that Ida was a special girl.

Now, she thought of all the times she and Ida laughed together, sharing a moment of levity amidst the chores, while Lavina and Hannah looked on from a distance. Of course they would want that same kind of connection with her.

Silently, she began to weep.

"I'm so dumb," she said softly.

His arms tightened. "No, no, dear heart. No, you are not. You have your hands full, and I could be a help to you by mentioning only what I have observed. You know we will both always be drawn to our own children, the ones we raised as babies. We saw them being born, we cherished their tiny faces, the way all parents do.

"But we have to keep trying to do the best we can. I noticed Suvilla is having problems, but to tell you the truth, Annie, I feel totally useless in helping her. She hardly says two words to me, and I can't think of anything to say to her. So now look who's dumb."

"Suvilla? I had no idea. Oh my word, Dan. It has nothing to do with you, at all. She's just at the age where she has no confidence, where everything looks scary and unsure. She'll be joining the *rumschpringa* in a few months, and that is a frightening time for many of us."

"But she doesn't like me."

"She will, once her life is more settled."

A comfortable silence fell between them, as they gently pushed back and forth on the old wooden swing. The crickets chirped continuously, the half-moon hung above them to the east, bathing the farm in its soft glow.

"Annie?"

"Yes."

"We'll work this all out in time, won't we?"

"Of course. I love how easily I can talk to you about anything. If we can continue to do that, I see no reason why things can't be normal soon enough. Christmas. I'll give it till Christmas," Annie laughed, trying to feel as confident and she made herself sound.

"Can you imagine all the gifts? And all the Christmas dinners we'll have to go to? This one at home, my family on both sides, and your family on both sides. That's five Christmas dinners, Annie."

"What fun!" she answered.

"Now you sound like Ida."

She laughed.

Dan shook his head, looking sober again.

"Lavina is so much like her mother, I'm afraid. Just full of . . . well, whatever it was that drove her to be so miserable at times."

"Oh, but I'm so glad you've made me aware of it."

Dan yawned, stretched. Annie gave an answering yawn, and together they made their way into the house, and to the bed that was a haven for their weary selves.

They did not kneel by the side of their bed to pray, having done that with the fourteen children around the kitchen table. Sixteen people, on their knees, heads bent in various degrees of holiness, the gas light hissing softly as Dan's voice rose and fell, reading from the German book the prayer that sustained his faith.

After breakfast the next morning, Dan announced he and Annie would be going to the small town of Intercourse, the name implying the hub of a wheel, where many roads met, and that Ida and Lavina could ride along. Ida raised both arms and cavorted around the kitchen shouting her glee, while Lavina, intimidated by this display of excitement, watched with hooded eyes.

They took the spring wagon, sitting in the open air, the sun already hot on their backs, the open view around them an endless source of entertainment for Ida, who gave a loud opinion on all her observations. They had gone less than half a mile before she said Henry Miller's heifers had parasites.

Dan burst into a loud guffaw of laughter, his head thrown back as he slapped his knee.

"Whatever do you mean?" Annie gasped, appalled.

"Their coats are shaggy and they have ribs that show."

Dan nodded, then slanted Annie a look.

"You're probably right, Ida," he said.

Then it was, "Why do we have to wear a bonnet? They're so hot and I can't see a thing."

Lavina listened, said nothing.

"You saw Henry Miller's heifers."

"Keep your bonnet on. We don't go anywhere without them, you know that."

"I would change that rule if I was the bishop. Why doesn't he change it? He doesn't have to wear a bonnet."

The thought of old Joas Stoltzfus wearing a bonnet, his white beard tucked beneath the strings, was more than Dan could picture in his mind without the benefit of a good laugh.

Annie smiled, but said sternly, "Ida, shame on you for talking that way."

When they reached the town of Intercourse, they turned off to the left and pulled up beside a few more teams tied to the hitching rack in the back of Zimmerman's Grocery and Hardware. Dan leaped off the wagon and tied the sorrel horse securely to the hitching post before turning to extend a hand to Annie. The girls clambered down by themselves, then stood brushing the fronts of their dresses and aprons for any stray horse hairs before following their parents into the store.

The floorboards creaked as they walked along the aisles, looking at various objects they might need. Ida and Lavina walked behind their parents, careful not to touch the stacks of rope or leather halters, cakes of soap, bags of cornmeal, new buckets and brooms, colorful bolts of fabric.

The proprietor of the store was small and wiry, with a shining bald head that appeared to be varnished like a good hardwood floor. He smiled at Dan and Annie, greeted them with a "Hello, folks," then turned to Ida and Lavina.

"And how are the girls?"

Ida replied for both of them. "We're fine, thank you."

They bought fifty pounds of flour, five pounds of white sugar, coffee, tea, baking powder and soda, a small measure of raisins, and a bag of licorice sticks for the children. Dan talked with the store clerk for a long time after paying for his purchases, discussing the president, the Depression, the state of the political party they agreed with, and what would become of the United States if Mr. Roosevelt didn't do something.

Annie took the girls out to the spring wagon where they sat waiting obediently, the sun climbing higher with increasing heat.

"Well, if I have a husband, he's not going to stand around talking to bald-headed English men while I sit in the sun," Ida announced.

Lavina surprised Annie when she said, "You might never have a husband."

Even Ida was speechless. Annie turned to find the

two black bonnets turned toward each other, with no sound coming from either one.

Finally, Ida lifted a shoulder.

"Well," she said. "You might not either."

"Oh. I plan on it, though."

Annie smiled to herself. It was a very small beginning, but it was one. Lavina was speaking her own mind.

When Dan appeared, he was sober, his expression troubled.

Annie turned to him with questioning eyes, but he shook his head.

"You need rolled oats, right?" he asked.

"I do."

"Then it's off to Rohrer's," he said, untying the horse, climbing up into the spring wagon, drawing back steadily on the reins till the horse backed against the britchment strap, pushing the spring wagon backwards.

"*Komm na*," he called softly, and the horse trotted off easily.

After that ride in the spring wagon, a new friendship began to develop between Ida and Lavina. By the time school started the first week in September, Lavina was like an unplugged drain, or an opened faucet, words that had been buried under sorrow and confusion now flowing freely.

The leaves turned various shades of yellow, orange, and red. It was the time of year when frost lay heavily in the hollows, withering the marigolds and petunias. Every tree was dressed in brilliant finery until a cold, slanting rain sent most of the leaves to the lawn below. The wind blew, wailing in from the north, and sent most of the leaves spinning off and away, so that there weren't too many to rake and burn at the end of the day.

Eleven children walked to school. Eleven lunchboxes were packed away every morning. Enos and Amos were in eighth grade, so this would be their last year, Annie thought, as she spread butter on eleven slices of bread, folded them, and wrapped them in waxed paper. Eleven sugar cookies and eleven apples. She had taken to baking the sugar cookies to a larger size, as the growing boys were all ravenous by the time they got home.

Every child went to school in bare feet, saving their shoes for the coming cold weather. With the frost on the ground, the calloused soles of their feet were cold, but not uncomfortably so, seeing how the sun warmed the earth before the first recess bell.

Joel and Lydia were in first grade, so that left only three-year-old Rebecca at home with Suvilla and Annie. The house was empty, the footsteps and footprints gone quiet, the shout and murmurs, the banging of doors and clattering of spoons absent, so that Annie said to Suvilla it seemed as if she couldn't breathe in this quiet air.

"Well, Mam. I for one, am happy to have them out of the way," she answered.

"Yes, we will get more accomplished, for sure."

The time of fall housecleaning was upon them, and every good Amish housewife took it seriously. No window could go unwashed, no walls or ceiling, and certainly no floor, left unscrubbed.

They lugged heavy buckets of scalding hot water up the stairs, then the second flight to the attic. Crates and cardboard boxes were pulled out from under the eaves, organized and cleaned, the floor underneath swept and scrubbed with hot lye soap and water. Windows were washed until they seemed polished.

No matter that no one would even set foot in Annie's attic. The dirt and spiderwebs weighed heavily on her conscience. What if one of them were to pass away and the community would descend on them like so many worker bees, cleaning, moving furniture, preparing the house for a funeral? It was a morbid thought, but it had happened to her once and it could happen again. Of course, if one of them were to die suddenly, the cleanliness of their home would not be forefront in her mind. But still, she always felt better having a clean and tidy house and knowing she was prepared for anything—as much as one can be, anyway.

Bucket after bucket of water was carried up the stairs, until the water turned dark gray with the dust and grime that always clung to the hewn floorboards. They surveyed their accomplishment with satisfaction. Even the sullen Suvilla seemed to find a hint of pleasure in the clean smell of the attic.

"Suvilla, when you have your own house, always remember I taught you how to clean an attic well," Annie remarked.

"I'll never have my own house," she huffed, her face taking on a deep shade of red.

Annie shook her head. "Oh, sure you will."

That ended the conversation. Suvilla had just joined the group of *rumschpringa*, and Annie knew she felt self-conscious about it. She was becoming quite a beautiful young woman, but if Suvilla felt humble about her appearance, it was best. Annie did not want a *grosfeelich* daughter who thought well of her own looks. How was a young girl to be discreet, a keeper at home, loving her husband, if she was puffed up with her own sense of vain glory? If Suvilla despised the breakouts on her skin, so be it. If she had only one Sunday dress and her friends had two or three, it could not be helped. Dan was a wonderful provider, but Annie was not about to waste money on fabric for dresses that the girls didn't really need.

How well she remembered her own time of *rumschpringa*, when she felt unworthy of any attention from young men. She was so deeply honored to have Eli Miller take notice of her and found it astounding that he should ask to come visit her that first Sunday evening.

Her wedding day had been every young girl's dream, and if Eli was less than perfect with the ambition that drove him, the quick temper and frequent needs, well, she wasn't perfect, either. She just had no idea back then, that any man could be what Dan was. Indeed, her year of grief, the crying for a night, had turned to the joy that came in the morning, just as the Bible promised. God had blessed her through her sorrow, the loss of the barn, so that He could lift her up to the height and strength of Dan's gentle love.

Even now, as she prepared a hasty lunch of buttered bread and bean soup, she waited eagerly for his step on the porch. He always met her eyes, that slow smile spreading across his kind face, as he asked how her work was coming along. She could trust him, trust that things would never change. His love was a beautiful thing.

She wished the same for Suvilla. She prayed that God would change her sullen nature. Yes, her father had passed away when she was a tender age, but many others went through the dark valley of sorrow. It was up to Suvilla to give herself up to whatever God chose to place before her, and the sooner she started to realize this, the better.

Chapter Nine

THE COLD WAS BECOMING MORE PRO-
nounced, so that shoes were brought out, handed
down, or new ones bought. After Thanksgiving,
there were coats to sew, mittens to crochet, scarves to
knit, so Annie was kept busy simply providing for the
children's needs. But the house cleaning was accomplished now, the yard raked and manure put on the
flower beds. The garden lay dormant under a cover
crop of fall oats, and the harvest was all down cellar
except for the cabbage and carrots.

No one went hungry, with plenty of milk from
the cows, cup cheese and cottage cheese, butter and
cold buttermilk. There were only enough eggs to sell
in the fall of the year, selling for a dollar a dozen,
which was phenomenal, according to Dan.

"You keep the egg money for Christmas gifts," he
told Annie.

"Oh, it's too much," she said, wide-eyed.

"No, I want you to get each child a nice present. Something special."

"*Ach*, well," was all she could think to say.

"They have all come a long way. None of this was easy for any of them. . . ."

"Except Ida," Annie reminded him.

"Except Ida," Dan laughed, shaking his head.

The egg money was put in a small dish on a shelf in the kitchen. All week she felt guilty as she returned from their trips to neighboring homes, pulling the old express wagon with egg boxes placed carefully in a cardboard box. She delivered eggs to the homes of several local English families, knocking on their doors, taking their money in exchange for the fresh eggs.

A dollar a dozen is not right, Annie thought for the hundredth time. The English families were hit by the Depression just as hard, if not harder, than the Amish community. The Amish families knew, at least, that they could turn to each other or to the church if they became desperate. Many of the English families did not have that kind of tight-knit community to support them.

"They don't have to buy these eggs," Dan assured her. "They want them, so if they pay a dollar, that's up to them. We're only making them available."

"But I feel as if I'm taking the money they should have to buy Christmas gifts."

"*Ach* Annie, now don't worry. If they want to buy eggs from someone else for less money, they can."

She had so many dollar bills, she decided to buy the candied fruit, nuts, raisins, and a brandy to make fruit cakes for Christmas. If she could sell a few cakes, it would make her feel better, as if she had at least earned the money that kept piling up in the dish.

The first snow arrived on the tenth of December, whirling hard little bits of ice on an Arctic wind that took her breath away that morning on her way to the barn for a jug of milk. She drew her scarf across her face, shivered, and slammed the milk house door. She stopped and held very still. From the cow stable came the sound of many voices, rising and falling, punctuated by ripples of laughter, a few lines of a silly song, carried along by the moist, acrid air that hung over a cow stable on a winter morning. She felt the rise of emotion in her throat. She walked toward the stable, a quick wave of gratitude formed the beginning of tears. *Thank you, Father.*

Here were her children and his children—Suvilla, Ephraim, Enos and Ida, Amos and Lavina—milking cows, forking hay, working together and seemingly having the time of their life.

"Hey, get over there, you dumb cow!"

"Watch it!"

She heard a clunking sound and knew a cow had placed a well-aimed kick and sent the bucket flying. Annie poked her head around the door to see a disgruntled Ephraim sprawled on his backside, with Ida standing in the aisle bent double slapping her knees with pure glee.

"There's manure on your pants!" she shrieked.

Suvilla poked her head out from between two cows, ready to restore order, then spied Ephraim and burst out laughing.

Annie backed away without having been noticed and made her way to the house through the whirling white snow.

Christmas was in the air with that first snowfall, so fruitcake making began in earnest. She had learned the art from her sister, the mixing, baking with a pan of water in the oven, the finished product wrapped and set in the pantry until the spices blended perfectly with the fruit and nuts. The children cracked walnuts and hickory nuts in the evening, and Annie stored them in glass jars. They would be used for cookies and cake throughout the year. Everything that grew on trees or in the garden was stored away. Chestnuts were roasted and eaten around the kitchen stove in the evening, although the children weren't allowed to eat all they wanted. Chestnuts could produce a stomachache.

There were two turkeys left in the barnyard, strutting around with their heads tucked in, their long beards wobbling across their puffed out chests. Joel and the two Emmas teased them with broomsticks, then ran howling in fear when one of them charged, the tail spread like a huge white fan, the pink eyes baleful.

Ida said if they didn't quit that they weren't going to be allowed to have *roasht* at the Christmas

dinner, but they didn't care. That is, until one afternoon a disgruntled goose chose to protect his barnyard friends and hissed in the farthest corner of the
fence, while the broomstick was making its rounds.
The children took no notice, until the wings were
spread, the long neck was lowered to a few inches
above the ground, the wide yellow feet propelled the
powerful body, and Joel was attacked with all the
force of a twenty-pound, very aggravated goose. The
strong yellow beak latched onto two of his fingers,
the young bones snapping like twigs, producing a yell
of mammoth proportion.

"Ow! Ow!" he screamed, clutching the injured
hand with the other. The two Emmas took one look
and ran on their skinny legs until they reached the
fence, scrambled up and over, falling down the other
side, to turn and peer between the boards with hor-
rified eyes.

"Is he dead?" Emma Two whispered.

"Not yet," Emma One hissed back.

His yells of pain and outrage brought Dan to the
cow stable door, then running to his son who was
clearly in mortal pain. Joel was taken to Doctor Hess in

New Holland, sniffling beside his father on the buggy seat, every bump in the road causing more discomfort. The doctor set the two fingers, taped them to a wooden splint, and told him to stay away from the geese in the barnyard. He charged Dan nothing, saying he'd pick up a bag of potatoes when he was in the area. Dan was grateful, thanked the kind doctor with a handshake, and led his chastened son back to the buggy.

As the horse clopped along through the wintry landscape, Dan looked down at Joel and asked if he thought they should put the two geese into *roasht* for Christmas dinner instead of the turkeys. Joel nodded solemnly.

They dressed in their best everyday clothes, Dan wearing his black Sunday hat. Annie had her heavy shawl pinned over a winter coat, and she wore two pairs of stockings and her rubber boots pulled on over her sturdy black shoes. The day was cold and bright, the sun's rays turning the snowy landscape into a blinding white world capped by a dome of blue. The horse trotted eagerly, the harness stirring up little puffs of dust as it jiggled on the horse's winter coat, thick and coarse.

Annie sat contentedly, leaning against her husband's solid strength, tucked into the buggy with a heavy lap robe, watching the winter scenery through the glass window. She had money to buy Christmas gifts, and found it almost unbelievable. Dan assured her that the children deserved this, every one, and it was not wrong in God's eyes to give gifts that brought joy to a child's face.

Annie nodded, but couldn't seem to silence her mother's disapproving voice in her head. But Dan was her husband, and he was the one she would honor and obey. Obeying him was the easiest task ever, the way he was so gentle and easygoing, so thoughtful of her. And so she tried her best to enjoy the day, to stop the feelings of guilt, that voice in her head that swam around like a repetitive goldfish, gurgling *No, no, no, you shouldn't, you can't, no, no no, it isn't right, it isn't right.*

She chuckled to herself, hadn't realized she made a sound till her husband smiled, looked down at her.

"What?" he asked, his eyes already crinkling in the corners.

"Nothing."

"It was something."

"Just thinking what my mother would say about this Christmas shopping."

"Didn't she buy Christmas gifts?"

"No."

"Not at all?"

"Oh no. Gifts are not necessary except giving up our own will to the Christ child."

His eyebrows went up, then lowered.

"Well, I suppose everyone is entitled to their own opinion. But for me, Christmas is a special time, especially for the children. And this year . . ."

Annie looked at him with a question in her eyes, amazed to find his mouth working to keep his emotion in check. For a long moment, silence filled the buggy.

Then he spoke. "Annie, you and the children are my Christmas gift this year. I am blessed far beyond anything I have ever imagined. You are so good, so beautiful, so . . . well, friendly and sweet. I have the best wife in the whole of Lancaster County."

She raised her eyes to his, her heart and soul drinking in every word.

"Thank you," she whispered brokenly.

How often she was weary, discouraged. How many nights did she fight the feeling of unworthiness before an uneasy slumber overtook her, only to awaken to the beating of her own heart, a staccato sound of primal fear of failure. But if this was how her husband felt, then this was what she would use to keep those moments at bay. His love was priceless, pillars that would support her forever.

They bought a new scarf and gloves for Sammy, both made of gray wool that would look sharp with his black coat and hat as he drove his spirited horse in the courting buggy. Dan said he often wished he could have known her when she was young, courted her the way Sammy would court a young lady soon.

For Suvilla there were four yards of red fabric to turn into a new Sunday dress and a handkerchief to match. "It's too much," Annie breathed, but Dan assured her that it would be good for Suvilla to having something new to wear, that a boost of confidence might draw her out of her dark mood.

Enos, Amos, and Ephraim would each receive a slingshot made from sturdy wood and rubber, along

with a pair of wool socks to keep their feet warm
when they skated on the pond. Dan said he'd probably regret buying those slingshots, but he knew they
would be pleased.

Lavina, Hannah, Ida, and the two Emmas would
all receive a tiny china tea set, each one in a different
pattern, to set on their dressers in the bedrooms they
shared, to hold and to admire.

They would all receive a handkerchief with a red
poinsettia design, their very own Christmas handkerchief to take to the Christmas dinners, the envy of all
the cousins.

Lydia and Rebecca would each be receiving a new
doll with such a pretty face it almost looked real little
girl. Annie had never seen such a doll, and had certainly
never considered purchasing one. She looked up at Dan.

"Are you sure these are not *app schtellt*?"

"What? A doll? Now why would they be forbidden? And I don't much care if they are. The little
girls need a nice doll."

Annie knew Dan was a bit liberal, but not quite to
this extent. But it wouldn't be right for her to question him again, so she smiled and nodded.

All her life, she had never owned a doll, not even a homemade rag doll. Her mother said they were idols, likeness made by man, teaching little girls to worship a manmade object. So she had poked holes in the largest corn cob she could find—two eyes, a nose, and a mouth—put her handkerchief on the head and another wrapped around the body, named her Veronica, and loved her with all her heart.

But this? This was too much. Yet she harbored a secret joy to think of Christmas morning.

Joel and John were not on the list, as Dan was carving and painting wooden horses and a wagon for them. He worked on the project for an hour or so every evening, sitting by the kitchen stove with a cardboard box on the floor to catch the shavings, his shoulders hunched in concentration.

It was those times when she wanted to tell him over and over how much she loved him, his solid, stable ways, his constant good humor. Would she never hear him kick his boots in a corner, slam a drawer, tug the roller towel that certain way that told her he was in a black mood? With Eli, she was often left wondering if she'd done—or not done—something to cause him to become so upset. And yet she had loved him wholeheartedly, never regretting their union.

Perhaps Dan and Annie had both been through the fire, had been shaped and molded and polished by their Creator, who worked in everyone's life until they shone in His image.

Whatever the reason, she walked up to Dan every evening, put her arms around his solid strength, and quietly laid her head on his back as he bent over the carving. There were no words, and none were necessary.

On the way home, the parcel containing Christmas gifts stowed under the back seat, Dan asked if she would like to stop for a visit to her grandmother, old Lizzie King. Annie could feel the hesitation before she quickly agreed. No need to let Dan in on all that.

"Yes, yes, of course."

She felt as if she was too loud and too eager, but was relieved when Dan merely smiled, her inner thoughts gone undetected.

Water under the bridge, she assured herself. All is gone and forgotten. She could not have prepared herself for the clenching in her chest as Dan guided the horse into the long lane that led to her grandparent's home.

Her mother's mother, her own blood relative, living out her years alone at the age of ninety-six.

Annie felt her heart quicken as they passed the old woodshed. No matter how desperately she had tried to do everything right, how many times had she been led to the woodshed strewn with shavings and slivers of bark, the smell of split wood, kerosene, and sawdust stinging her nose. It was there that her grandmother whipped her, the slice of the thin iron rod like a knife against her bare legs. It was only when she finally cried out, begged her to stop, that the rod was stilled, set in the corner to mock her own weakness, while her grandmother told her if she ever told her mother, there would be another whipping twice as bad.

Annie had never breathed a word of it.

These things must be forgotten, forgiven, buried forever in the haunted archives of human nature. Perhaps this was what she herself had experienced at the hand of her own grandmother, or mother, perhaps her own father. Who knew? Better to leave it buried, stomped beneath the fertile soil of forgiveness, the soil that God would nurture, heal with the growth of beautiful flowers and grasses, where butterflies and bees could drink their fill of sweet nectar.

To summon the courage to walk through the old door was a real test, to walk across the pine-boarded floor and shake the gnarled old hand, to allow the near blind eyes to search her face with recognition, a superhuman effort.

"Oh, Annie. It's you."

"Grandmother, this is Dan," she said, her voice weaker than she wanted it to be.

Slowly, the head turned; the rheumy old eyes watered to focus.

"Ya, ya. I heard you married again."

"Yes. I did."

"Fourteen children you have."

"Yes."

The old face crumpled; a claw-like hand searched in a dress pocket for a handkerchief as dry rasps of sound came from the ridged old throat.

"Be nice to them. Be nice to the children."

It was the last thing Annie expected to hear.

"Oh, we are. We try to be."

"Gute. Gute. Annie, I'm sorry . . . for, you know
. . ." She began to cry then, one slow tear down her
wrinkled cheek.

"*Ach*, Grandmother. Don't cry," Annie said, touched
and confused by the sudden display of emotion.

There was so much more to say, but somehow,
the words didn't really matter. Annie took her grandmother's hand and held it, and that was enough.

On the way home, Dan asked gently what that
had all been about. Annie found herself telling him
everything, the words opening a locked room in her
heart, tears flowing freely in the cold breeze. When
she was done, she felt like a weight had been lifted
from her chest.

Dan let her speak, listening in compassionate
silence, placing an arm around her shoulder and
drawing her close when she began to weep.

"There's one more thing," she said, looking down
at her lap.

"What's that?" he asked softly, almost a whisper.

"Sometimes . . ." She choked back a sob before
continuing. "Sometimes I lose my patience, or I feel

coldhearted toward our children, Dan. And I wonder if I am no better than my grandmother was to me. Dan, I'm afraid I don't deserve a kindhearted man like you."

He slowed the horses and turned his face toward her, looking very serious. They were on a quiet side road now, away from traffic and houses. "Annie, you cannot believe that," he said, with a voice that was deep, gentle, but firm. "You mustn't. You are exactly what our children need. You are kind and loving and wise. You are exactly what *I* need."

He pulled the horses to a stop. Annie turned her face toward his, searching his eyes and finding every evidence that he meant the words with his whole heart.

"Annie, no one is perfect—it is God who works through us to give us strength and goodness and love. But you, Annie . . . you are about as perfect as a woman can be. You are just right for our family, just right for me. I love you, Annie."

He leaned down and kissed her tears away, flooding her with a warmth and freedom she had never before known.

Chapter Ten

HOW COULD ANNIE FULLY DESCRIBE THE delight and anticipation with which she wrapped the gifts in newspaper and tied them with string?

She had never given Christmas gifts such as these, never spent money on a gift for her children. Sometimes, Eli had purchased a bag of oranges, or a small sack filled with hard candies, but never had she has much as imagined spending egg money for anything other than basic necessities, or handing it to Eli to help with the payment for the farm. She battled her guilt, from time to time, until she confided in Dan, and he again told her the Lord wanted to give his children happiness, things to enjoy, and gradually Annie allowed herself to accept his views. He even showed her the verse in the Bible that spoke of Jesus giving abundant life to His followers. "Of course you can live abundantly without possessions," he said, "but there is nothing wrong with enjoying God's physical blessings in our lives."

As if that extravagance wasn't enough, they made another trip to town to buy supplies for candy and cookies, pies and cakes. They met acquaintances, stopped to visit outside Zimmerman's grocery, shared news in the parking lot by the hitching rack in the cold gray air, the women clutching their black woolen shawls around their bodies, the men settling their black hats more firmly as the cold breeze toyed with the brims.

Becky Zook was a small, rotund woman with a face like a round, glistening plum. Her cheeks bobbed and wagged against the sides of her black bonnet as she spoke, her eyes darting from Dan's face to Annie's. "My oh, it's good to see you out and about together. I haven't been able to visit yet, which is no excuse. I'm sure you wondered where I was all this time."

Annie assured her it was quite all right. She didn't say out loud that her absence hadn't even crossed her mind. She hardly knew the woman.

"We live across the Pequea from you. Our land borders Elam and Rachel's farm. You know, Elam Beiler. They have that poor child."

"Oh, yes. We go to the same church. Yes, of course."

"See, they just divided our district a while back. Before you married Dan."

Here she stepped up and placed a gloved hand on Annie's forearm, her eyes filling with tears like two wet diamonds, the love and concern as priceless.

"I can't tell you how glad I am he has a wife. He did his best all those years, and presented a brave face to the rest of us, but I can't imagine what the poor man has seen in his life. You know his first wife was *opp im kopp*, don't you?"

Annie's eyes went to her husband uneasily. Here was a subject as prickly as a cactus. It felt far too much like gossip, and gossiping about her husband's late wife seemed especially wrong.

"But she was, you know. She was never quite right in the head."

She persisted until Annie said, quietly, "I am sure God had mercy and understanding for her condition."

Becky nodded, then tilted her head to one side, and pursed her lips. "The pneumonia was a mercy. I was always afraid she would . . ."

And here she stepped even closer, her breath a hot wave of half-digested food ". . . end it all by her own hand. And everyone knew those kinds of people are not buried in the cemetery, but outside the fence."

She stepped back, her eyes on Annie's face, watching her response.

"Well, God's ways are not our ways," was all Annie could think to say.

"*Ach*, yes, yes of course. Well, I do admire your attitude about it. Now tell me, how are the children doing? Do you find it hard to accept Dan's boys?"

"The children are doing well, really."

She ignored the second question, more anxious than ever to escape the conversation. She was relieved when Dan turned, asked if she was ready to go.

They bought white sugar and food coloring, boxes of confectionery sugar and chocolate, cocoa powder and coconut, all luxury items that were unnecessary, but Annie's protests did no good. Behind the cereal aisle, he told her if she didn't hush up, he would kiss her and he didn't care who saw them, either.

They were laughing together, Annie's face flushed with pleasure, when they ran into her mother, her face white and drawn, her lips pursed in distaste.

"Oh, Mam, how are you?" Annie asked breathlessly.

"Good. And you?"

"We are good," Dan answered.

"Well, I would imagine Annie can speak for herself," was her tart reply.

"I am well, Mam."

"Well, the children are adjusting, I presume."

"Yes, they are."

"I must be along. I am in town for chicken feed."

Mercifully, her black bonnet was drawn well over her face, like the blinders on a horse's bridle, and she could not see the bulging shopping bag in Dan's hand.

On the way home, a comfortable silence stretched between Dan and Annie, each lost in their own thoughts, not in a troubled fashion, but contemplating the great worth of community and friends. The ability to come and go as they pleased, the religious freedom the Amish enjoyed, and what the forefathers had done to establish this way of life.

The task of raising the fourteen children seemed daunting, but with God's help and guidance, it would be possible for all of them to keep the faith, to continue the plain way of life.

The cookie and candy making began in earnest in the week before Christmas. After the children went off to school (would she ever become used to packing eleven lunches?), she sat with Suvilla and went through all her recipes. Molasses cookies were Dan's favorites, and the ones with the least expensive ingredients. Sugar cookies would be replaced by sand tarts, which were thinner than sugar cookies but could still be cut into shapes with the aluminum cookie cutters, brushed with beaten egg, and dotted with raisins or colored sugar. There would be soft cookies with apples and nuts, glazed with a thin white frosting, also sprinkled with sugar. Oatmeal cookies would be next, and finally chocolate cookies with confectioner's sugar sprinkled across the tops.

They would make a cake roll, filled with strawberry jam. Then a huge three-layer nut cake made with the walnuts from the black walnut tree in the backyard, covered in brown sugar icing flavored with maple syrup. And for pies there would be mincemeat, pumpkin, and apple-raisin.

Suvilla's cheeks were flushed with anticipation, the sullen, rebellious look gone for now. The kitchen was awash in wintery sunlight and the promise of all the sweets they would soon be making. Suvilla loved to cook and bake, and she was good at it—she mixed bread dough with the best, and set cakes on the counter that always turned out light and airy.

"So, what do you suggest we start first?" Annie asked. Suvilla glanced at her mother, a challenge returning to her eyes.

"Why ask me? It's up to you."

"Not just me. We can decide together."

"If I was the boss—which I'm not, of course—I'd do everything but the sand tarts. You chill the dough outside, right?"

Annie nodded.

"Then maybe the little ones can help when they come home from school. What do you think?"

"An excellent idea, Suvilla. That is thoughtful of you, and I appreciate that so much."

Suvilla flushed, rose to her feet self-consciously, then bent to retrieve the large bowl she would be using to mix the molasses cookies. Annie watched her face, amazed to find her oldest daughter blinking away tears. She must remember to praise her more, she thought.

The house was filled with the smell of sugar and cinnamon, molasses and ginger. Sheets of cookies were emptied onto a clean white tablecloth, the kitchen range keeping a steady heat as they controlled the fire with just the right amount of wood, a skill perfected by years of experience. As the sun warmed the cold, snowy landscape, the temperature in the kitchen climbed steadily, until they admitted it was uncomfortable and opened a window to allow in a cooling draught.

When Dan came in for lunch, he was handed a cold ham sandwich with a cup of tea and told to taste test the cookies. He laughed and admitted to hoping they would give him that job. Annie marveled yet again at how easy it was to be with Dan. With Eli, he might have praised her for all her hard work, or he might have been in a dark mood and eaten lunch quickly before storming back outside to continue his work, leaving Annie to wonder if he disapproved of her baking.

It was only Suvilla being in the kitchen that kept Annie from putting her arms around Dan and telling him how much she appreciated his steady good nature. Annie had come to see that Suvilla had a problem with her adoration of her new husband. Perhaps Suvilla felt her mother was too happy, a bit loose with her show of love. Did she think Annie had moved on too quickly after Eli's death?

For the thousandth time, Annie whispered a prayer for the Lord to show her the way, to bless her navigation through the treacherous path of being a mother and stepmother. But this time, Dan's reassuring words echoed in her mind, reminding her that reaching for perfection would only lead to despair. She told God she would never be perfect, but that He had placed her here and so she trusted that He would help her through the tough times. She thanked Him for Dan's gentle love and asked Him to keep knitting their family together.

When the whole flock of children clattered into the washhouse after school, kicking boots into corners, hanging coats, hats, and bonnets haphazardly across hooks, flinging scarves and mittens in the general direction of the cardboard box meant to hold them all, Annie found herself braced for the chaos that would be sure to follow. She was grateful Suvilla had had the foresight to pack most of the cookies away in tins so they'd be out of sight, leaving only a few plates of assorted cookies on the table.

"Cookies!" Ida yelled, her normal exuberance elevated to hysteria. Not to be outdone, the two Emmas and Lydia ran in circles, lifted both arms in a hallelujah dance of joy, while Joel and John promptly leaped onto the table and gathered handfuls of molasses and oatmeal.

"No, no, no, no," Suvilla said loudly above the general hubbub. She grabbed them both by one arm and hauled back. They howled in protest, which brought Annie to the scene, telling them to replace the cookies and wash their hands first.

Amos, Ephraim, and Enos remembered their manners, and stood with hands in their pockets, feigning disinterest, before asking in gruff voices how many they were allowed to have.

Glasses of milk were poured, and Annie stood back, watching helplessly as the cookies disappeared before her eyes. It seemed like a matter of seconds before the tabletop was sadly depleted.

"Well, children," Annie said.

"What?"

"All of our cookies are gone!" she wailed in mock despair.

Faces were lifted with howls of glee, swift denials in the form of "I only had two!" followed by fair accusations of the truth. It was absolute bedlam. Finally Suvilla shouted over the din that she was going to get the washing off the line, that it was hopeless in here.

After the milk was drained from eleven tumblers, the last cookie crumb eaten, they were all dispatched to their various chores, leaving little Rebecca and Joel to amuse themselves with the wooden blocks till suppertime.

Annie made a big pot of beef stew, hastily cutting up potatoes, carrots, cabbage, and onion, with chunks of beef and the soup bone to flavor it all, then added the savory dumplings. This was served with applesauce and small green pickles, slabs of bread and molasses.

As she ladled the thick, rich stew on to the children's plates, she couldn't imagine how they could possibly be hungry after all those cookies, but they spooned up the thick stew, crunched the small pickles, and asked for seconds. The cold had turned their cheeks red, and now, by the warmth from the kitchen range, the faces turned even brighter, the many pairs of eyes glistening with the beginning of nightly fatigue.

Dishes were washed and the chilled sand tart dough brought in from the back porch, amid cries of appreciation and rolling pins held aloft like weapons. The older boys helped Dan with the milking, saying they wanted no part of cookie making, which was for girls and sissies, which brought Ida's hands to her narrow hips and a glare to her eyes that could have felled a cat.

Hannah told the boys they were just jealous, that they wished they were allowed to help with the baking. Annie watched the boys' eyes open wide in disbelief at this bit of truthful insight from the bashful Hannah, then clunk out to the washhouse where they pulled on their boots, asking each other what had come over Hannah to make her so bold all of a sudden.

Ida gave Hannah a gleeful smile, and Hannah batted her eyelashes and stepped up to the table, grabbed a rolling pin, and prepared to roll out the dough, which turned out to be trickier than it appeared. She leaned over the table with all her weight, flattening the cold dough as far as much as she could. When she had practically broken a sweat, Suvilla stepped in and rolled until the dough was thin enough for the cookie cutters to be put to use. The colored sugar was an endless source of wonder for the two Emmas, who did all the decorating, except for the raisin eyes and buttons on the gingerbread men. That job went to Lydia, while Ida took it on herself to supervise everyone . . . which did not go over well.

Suvilla told her mildly to go away and mind her own business, clearly exercising great restraint in her choice of words.

Ida puffed up her chest, drew down her eyebrows, and snorted.

"Ida," Annie warned, lifting a Christmas tree with a metal spatula.

"Mam, Suvilla isn't using enough flour. Her dough is sticking to the tabletop. Tell her."

"You know, Ida, your chance of becoming an old maid keeps getting better each year," Suvilla said forcefully.

"You have no idea. What if I choose to stay single? Huh? Then what? You don't have anything to say to that, now, do you?"

"I don't care if you marry someone or not."

For once, Ida didn't have a reply to that. And then, because it was Christmastime, and everyone felt the spirit of happiness and goodwill, the tiff blew over before it became serious, though Annie suspected Ida would pursue it again the minute she was safely out of her hearing.

Between the long hours on her feet, the mixing and rolling and feeding the fire, and the noise and commotion of all the children, Annie had developed a pounding headache above her right eye. She had just finished the dishes and swept the floor and was about to put away the last ingredients when Joel, trying to be helpful, dumped green sugar all over the floor, then turned and walked through it.

It was an accident, it was an accident, she thought, over and over. But she could not bring herself to smile at him or tell him it was all right. *He needs to learn to be more careful. And all that sugar wasted!*

When he sat on the couch with his thumb in his mouth, his bright eyes watching every move she made, she still didn't feel the need to comfort him. When Dan came in to wash up he asked her where there was another cake of soap. She was short with him, telling him to look for it in the washhouse somewhere, instead of offering to help.

No, she was not perfect. But she no longer spiraled into the depths of guilt and despair. Instead, she asked God for forgiveness for her shortcomings and went to bed.

In the morning, breakfast over and the eleven off to school, her strength and good humor returned. She'd had a good night of sleep and an extra cup of coffee laced with the cream that lay thick and rich on top of a gallon of milk.

Oh, she was spoiled. She was becoming used to coffee as a morning necessity instead of a luxury, but it was so good—the thick, rich smell that made her close her eyes as she breathed deeply. She hummed German Christmas carols under her breath as her sturdy arms plied the crumbs for another batch of pie dough.

Suvilla ran down cellar and brought the canned pumpkin for the filling, then separated eggs and beat the egg whites to a stiff peak.

Annie mixed the chopped beef, the broth, and many spices that would create the mincemeat pies. They mixed apples and brown sugar, butter and cinnamon for the apple-raisin pies, poured it all into prepared crust, and baked them to a golden-brown perfection.

Annie showed Suvilla how she could tell when the pumpkin pies were baked hard enough. "Just take them and give them a gentle shake," she said. "They should shiver a little bit in the middle, but not too much."

"That's not very specific," Suvilla muttered, but watched carefully as her mother closed the oven door to allow them to bake awhile longer. "Let's finish all the Christmas baking before they all get home from school."

"Why?" Annie laughed.

"You know why," Suvilla said dryly.

"Oh my, what a mess!" Annie laughed. "But it was worth it, every sticky surface and ruined cookie was worth every minute. The children seemed like brothers and sisters, every last one. Did you hear Emma One tell Emma Two how her gingerbread man looked like Elam sie Rachel, and Emma Two laughed so hard she bumped her heard on the corner of the table? He did look like her, the way the raisins were placed close together, low on the face."

"Those two Emmas are a team, aren't they?"

"Kindred spirits, indeed."

Annie straightened, telling Suvilla she would not trade place with anyone else on earth. "This is where God wants me to be, so I guess he'll supply strength for each new day and all the problems that come with it."

"Yes, Mam, but things aren't quite as hard as it was at first. We all seem to grow together somehow." Here her eyes narrowed, and her face took on an iron resolve. "But I'll tell you one thing. I can hardly wait for a home of my own, a tiny house with no one in it except my husband and me."

"Your husband being Henry King's Aquilla, perhaps?"

Suvilla's mouth opened, then closed, as her face became infused with color.

"Mam! I am shocked! You know nothing about Aquilla King."

Annie nodded, smiled, and would not meet her daughter's eyes.

Chapter Eleven

ON CHRISTMAS EVE, DAN GATHERED ALL THE children into the living room. In his gentle, deep voice, he read the Christmas story to them all, in English, since the little ones had not yet learned the German. They sat quietly, all fourteen of them, some cross-legged on the floor, some doubled up on a comfortable chair, and the smallest ones on the couch with him. As his voice rose and fell, they seemed spellbound, absorbing every word. Sammy was listening, his face softened by emotion. Suvilla sat with her face showing nothing, her eyes downcast, but the fact that she was there gave Annie a warm feeling.

When the story was finished, there was a collective sigh, a few swipes of hands across tired eyes, a yawn here and there. But all waited, knowing Christmas Eve would not be over till the evening prayer was read from the German prayer book. They watched as Dan reached to the bookshelf, then all of them turned as one, got on their knees as Dan did, and buried their faces in crooked arms or simply gazed through chair rungs. Their minds churned with everyday things, as happens when the prayer is long and the singsong monotone keeps rising and falling.

Then the children straggled off to bed, weary from an afternoon of play. The snow had accumulated to eight or ten inches, so the steep hill in the cow pasture sported an icy track made by hundreds of boot prints, a log, and the use of many sleds. Faces were wind-chapped, lips peeling and blistered from the combination of wind and sun, but a dollop of Vaseline helped them all to sleep without pain. None of them had any idea of the Christmas presents that would be waiting for them in the morning. She had wrapped each package in newspaper and would set them on clean plates at the breakfast table.

Annie had made fresh shoofly pie, and there would be the luxury of hot chocolate to go with it, all the eggs and home cured ham they could hold, stewed crackers and fresh pancakes with maple syrup.

She had a hard time falling asleep that night, thinking of the two dolls, more than anything else. She had never imagined one of her children owning a store-bought doll, an item she had longed for with secret intensity when she was a child. She hoped they were not damaging the little girls by spoiling them with such a large Christmas gift.

The alarm jangled at five o'clock on Christmas Day, the same time Dan and Annie arose every morning. There were chores to do, water pipes to thaw, fires to stoke with chunks of wood. Annie had to put the two geese in the oven that she would be using to make the *roasht*, and beat the cream with the egg beaters to mix with the cornstarch pudding.

She dressed eagerly, then called the oldest children to go get the milking started. Then she tiptoed to the bedroom closet and carefully brought out each package and laid them tenderly on every child's plate, then stood back and surveyed the wonder of it. What would they say?

She turned to find Sammy sitting on the couch, pulling on his cotton socks. Then Suvilla stumbled into the kitchen, stopped, and stared.

Her eyes went to Annie's beaming face.

"We have gifts?"

"We do!"

"What is it?"

"Well Suvilla, it's Christmas, so I guess you'll have to wait and see."

Suvilla raised her eyebrows, then smiled genuinely. "Huh," was all she said.

Sammy smiled at his mother, then followed Suvilla to the washhouse to dress in warm clothes.

Enos, Ephraim, and Amos clomped down the stairs, in various forms of wakening, wiping eyes, yawning, their hair in a mess of tangles.

"It's cold," Enos complained.

Annie smiled. "Good morning, boys."

Amos spied the wrapped gifts. His eyes shot open, wide, then wider, "Gifts!"

Ephraim and Enos snapped to attention.

"We have Christmas gifts!" they said, their voices barely above a shocked whisper.

"Can we open them?"

"Not till breakfast. Now hurry and get your chores done."

They fell over each other getting to the washhouse and out the door to the barn, pulling wool hats down over their ears as they ran. The dark and the cold was ablaze with excitement for all of them.

At six, Annie woke the rest of the children, helping them to dress and comb their hair. She brushed out snarls, wet the top of six little girls' heads, her fingers flying as she used a fine-toothed comb to flatten the hair before deftly rolling along the sides to two coils in the back. Those coils were then wound around and around to form a perfect circular bob, pinned tightly with steel hairpins. There were no barrettes or rubber ponytail holders, simply the coils of hair rolled and pinned into place by years of practice.

Once downstairs, Ida caught sight of the wrapped presents, and for once in her life she was speechless. Lavina stood beside her, gaping, followed by Hannah, Lydia, and the two Emmas.

Annie could not stop smiling.

She fried slices of ham, set the milk to heat, then mixed the batter for the pancakes with a song in her head. Today was the day of the Christ child's birth, so why wouldn't she rejoice with the heavenly host of angels, the very same ones who sang over the hills of Judea where the shepherd watched their flocks, or the ones who hovered over the stable in Bethlehem? Here was cause for a deep and abiding joy, a spiritual renewal for mankind.

Oh, that He had been born and died for her! The fact of it lent wings to her feet, sent the song to her lips.

She was singing "Hark! The Herald Angels Sing" softly when she heard Ida joining in, her sweet voice soon overtaking her own as the song grew louder and faster, until she was up off the couch, head bobbing, feet skipping, then arms out as she twirled around the living room.

"Now, Ida, we don't approve of dancing. Especially not to a Christmas hymn."

"Why not? It's the happiest day of my life!"

Annie laughed outright.

"Why of course it is."

Ida's brows compressed into a serious wrinkle.

"So far, at least."

She looked thoughtful for a few moments, before saying, "But I plan on having many more happy days, Mam."

"You will, Ida. You certainly will."

A clattering in the washhouse heralded the arrival of the herd of workers from the barn. After that, it was undisguised chaos, the children cheering when Dan caught Annie by the waist for a great Christmas bear hug. The din was irreparable, with Dan's wide smile, Annie's blushing face, especially when she announced it was time to fry the eggs and Dan would not let her go.

The gas lights hissed, casting a yellowish glow over the warm kitchen and the steaming platters and bowls of food. The coffeepot boiled, sending the rich aroma through the house, the salty odor of frying ham mingled with the browned butter in the cast iron pan, waiting for the dropped eggs.

On Christmas Eve, there had been the solemn story of Christ's birth, but today was the celebration. Each child could feel the joy of the Christmas spirit as they slid into their respective seats, each one touching the wrapped present with hands that hesitated, allowing only the tips of their fingers to come into contact with the layers of newspaper.

The food was brought to the table, presents set on the floor beside them, till the plates could be taken away.

Was ever a Christmas morning quite like this one?

The eggs slid from the plate, nestled beside a thick slice of ham, a serving of stewed crackers, rich and milky, dotted with browned butter. Spoons and forks clattered against plates till every morsel was scraped clean. It was almost unimaginable to have a pancake afterward, soaked in butter and drizzled with maple syrup, followed by all the shoofly pie they could hold. A steaming cup of hot chocolate brought more cheers, which Ida led, her voice rising above everyone else's.

Dan lifted a spoonful of shoofly pie, dipped it below the surface of the hot cocoa, put it in his mouth, and closed his eyes.

"Mmm . . . Mmm . . ."

Annie smiled. "You like my shoofly pie?"

"You know I do. They're the best. Along with the prettiest wife in Lancaster County, I get shoofly pies that are unbelievable."

"Hurry up, Dat," said Ida. "We're finished. Time for presents."

Dan looked up, his eyes softened, and for one moment Annie was afraid he would shed real tears.

"You called me Dat," he said.

Ida smiled at him, flashing her mischievous dimple to its full extent.

"You are my dat, the only one I have."

Was that a nodding from Sammy and Suvilla?

They allowed the youngest to open her package first, with Dan and Annie's help. As the face of the doll emerged, Rebecca's eyes became round with surprise, then her face crumpled and she began to cry.

"What? What is this?" Annie asked, quickly gathering her for a close embrace on her lap.

"Don't cry, Rebecca."

Little Rebecca had never seen a store-bought doll, and was frightened by the eyes that opened and closed. So they had Lydia open her gift, who was so thrilled she simply let out a high shriek of delight, then turned to say quite solemnly, "*Denke*, Mam und Dat."

Everyone was on their feet, crowding around, helping Rebecca unwrap the doll, smoothing the tiny gathers in the dress, opening and closing the doll's eyes, moving the arms and legs. The boys pulled on the thin socks, and when one fell on the floor, they were faced with Lavina's outrage, Ida's yanking on their shoulders, and a frown of disapproval from Suvilla.

Rebecca held the doll then, but carefully, afraid to touch the pretty face or the glistening fabric of the dress.

Dan got up from his chair, asked Joel and John if they had not noticed their plates were empty.

"Yes, we did. But you have something for us," they said, almost as one person. Annie was touched to see the faith they had, trusting Dan would bring them their gift.

The wooden wagon was painted green, with yellow wheels and fine black pinstriping for the spokes and the rim. The attached horse was painted brown with a black harness. Annie had made small cloth bags filled with rice, to load on the wagons—little bags of feed for the horse to take to town.

It was all bedlam after that. Even Sammy was on the floor, delighted with the ease of the wheels' motion.

Enos, Amos, and Ephraim thought they should be next, until the girls reminded them they were younger, and opened their package to find the most remarkable thing they had ever seen. Awed by the delicacy of this fine china, they carried it to the dressers in their room to be handled and admired every day. They were now the owners of genuine china dishes, and they carried themselves with a new lift of their shoulders.

When the boys opened their present to find a slingshot, Annie detected a note of envy in Ida's voice. Amid the howls of glee, Ida told them they'd never be able to hit the side of a barn with those things.

As Annie suspected, she had the slingshots in her hands almost as much as the boys, and became a dead shot with it before the winter was over.

The wool socks were drawn over their feet, proclaimed the warmest things they'd ever worn, followed by heartfelt, effusive "*Denke Denke.*"

Suvilla opened her gift, her face an incredulous mask.

Her mouth opened and closed. She stroked the wonderful fabric, smooth and soft, folded and unfolded the handkerchief, then lifted her face with eyes like the twinkling of stars.

"It's too much," she said finally.

Annie tried to smile, but found her mouth turning down of its own accord, a stinging in her nose the imposter that brought unwanted tears.

Her beautiful oldest daughter, so young and unspoiled, having gone through so much in her short life. Only God knew how much she had suffered, and how much love and nurturing she would need.

Dan saw Annie's face, reached for her hand and squeezed, a heartfelt signal of his support, the priceless gift of his love.

Sammy grinned, tried on the scarf and gloves, said it was exactly what he needed, then blushed to the roots of his hair, thinking about asking a certain young lady to the Christmas singing. Ida said it looked as if that scarf was really warm as red as his face became after a while.

They sang Christmas songs, one after another. They played games—tic-tac-toe, dice, ring toss. They popped popcorn, buttered and salted it, drank cider and all the coffee they wanted.

Annie took the two geese from the blue agate roaster, deboned them, mixed the meat with bread

cubes, celery, onion, and eggs, popped it back into
the oven, and set the potatoes to boil. She roasted
squash, turnips, and sweet potatoes, and shredded
cabbage for pepper slaw. Suvilla set the table with
the best tablecloth, the good china, glass dishes of
shivering strawberry jam, dark green pickles, and
chow-chow. They shaped the warmed butter into
Christmas bells, opened jars of applesauce and grape
mush.

The dinner was eaten at three in the afternoon,
before chores.

The children were hungry, raking huge amounts
of *roasht* onto their plates, heaping spoonfuls of potatoes and gravy.

The black walnut cake was sliced and devoured
with scoops of creamy cornstarch pudding and
canned peaches. The mincemeat, cherry, and apple
pies were brought from the pantry amid groans of
protest.

Everything was just so plentiful, so rich and warm
and cozy. The fire crackled in the range, savory odors
wafted through the house, filling it with the sense of
goodwill. The children sat together, playing games,

admiring dolls, rattling horses and wagons across the floor, the security of having a mother and father watching over them.

The snow fell like a benediction that Christmas day, wrapped the house and barn in a soft, glistening blanket, covered the ground like a coating of grace, hiding the mud and weeds and sharp stones, the way Christ's gift covered the multitude of wrongdoings of men.

All this was not lost on Dan or Annie, as they got up to put another log on the fire, or to fill a glass with grape juice or a cup of coffee.

Bedtime was later; the children's begging produced results from contented parents who saw nothing wrong with an extension of this joyful day. When at last Annie spied John pushing his horse and wagon while lying prostrate on the floor, his heavy eyelids falling occasionally, she said it was time for the evening prayer, and then rose from her chair and shoed them all to bed, after the evening prayer.

Dan was sweeping the floor when she came back down the stairs, so she began picking up, sorting toys and gloves and socks. She washed dishes while he finished sweeping the kitchen, then grabbed a tea towel and started to dry them.

"Are you very tired?" he asked, in his soft voice.

"I shouldn't be. We sat around all afternoon," she said.

"Would you be interested in going for a walk with me?"

"A walk?"

"Yes, in the snow."

She didn't hesitate, thinking of the pure snow falling in a gray winter night when every sound was hushed, even footfalls whispered.

After bundling themselves in warm outerwear and heavy boots, they walked past the barn and outbuildings, down the field lane, until the whole world was a sea of white and gray, the snowflakes falling soundlessly as they fell to earth.

Dan stopped, took her shoulder, and turned her toward him, "Annie, I want to tell you now, on this blessed Christmas Day, that you are the best earthly gift I have ever received or even hope to receive in the future. You are an amazing woman."

She could think of no reply at all, so she said very soft and low, "Oh, Dan. *Ach.*"

He took her in his arms and kissed her gently, sealing his love for her now and forever.

The snow fell steadily on the farmhouse roof where fourteen children of various ages lay sleeping peacefully, content in the knowledge that they were family now, and would always be, as long as God allowed them to live on this good earth.

THE END

Glossary

Ach—Oh (an expression of surprise)
App schtellt—forbidden
Ausbund—German hymnal
Bowa feesich—bare feet
Die Englishy—the English (non-Amish people)
Doggie fils—a casserole made with sliced hot dogs and cubed bread
Glaeyne frau—my little wife
Greishas—yelling
Grosfeelich—haughty
Gute nacht, Kinna—Good night, children
Hausfrau—housewife
Hesslich—seriously
Kinna—children
Komm na—come now
Kommet—come
Maud—maid
Mold oh—Look here
Opp im kopp—mentally ill; literally, off in the head

Patties noona—Hands down, an expression meaning
   to pray before a meal
Rumschpringa—The period when young teenagers
   begin dating
Schnitza—lie
Unbekimmat—uncaring

About the Author

LINDA BYLER WAS RAISED IN AN AMISH FAMILY and is an active member of the Amish church today. Growing up, Linda loved to read and write. In fact, she still does. Linda is well known within the Amish community as a columnist for a weekly Amish newspaper. She writes all her novels by hand in notebooks.

Linda is the author of several series of novels, all set among the Amish communities of North America: Lizzie Searches for Love, Sadie's Montana, Lancaster Burning, Hester's Hunt for Home, The Dakota Series, and the Buggy Spoke Series for younger readers. She also wrote *The Healing* and *A Second Chance*, as well as several Christmas romances set among the Amish: *Mary's Christmas Goodbye*, *The Christmas Visitor*, *The Little Amish Matchmaker*, *Becky Meets Her Match*, *A Dog for Christmas*, and *A Horse for Elsie*. Linda has coauthored *Lizzie's Amish Cookbook: Favorite Recipes from Three Generations of Amish Cooks!*

OTHER BOOKS BY
LINDA BYLER

LIZZIE SEARCHES FOR LOVE SERIES

BOOK ONE   BOOK TWO   BOOK THREE

TRILOGY   COOKBOOK

SADIE'S MONTANA SERIES

BOOK ONE

BOOK TWO

BOOK THREE

TRILOGY

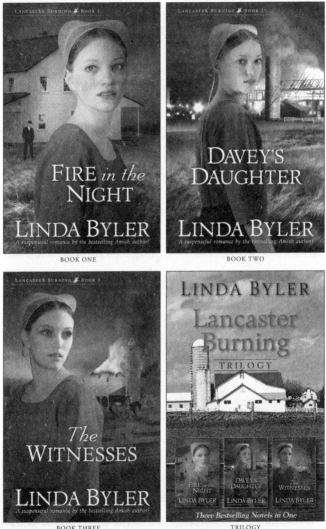

BOOK ONE

BOOK TWO

BOOK THREE

TRILOGY

BOOK ONE

BOOK TWO

BOOK THREE

TRILOGY

THE DAKOTA SERIES

The Homestead — Linda Byler
BOOK ONE

Hope on the Plains — Linda Byler
BOOK TWO

Home is where the Heart is — Linda Byler
BOOK THREE

Linda Byler — The Dakota Series TRILOGY
TRILOGY

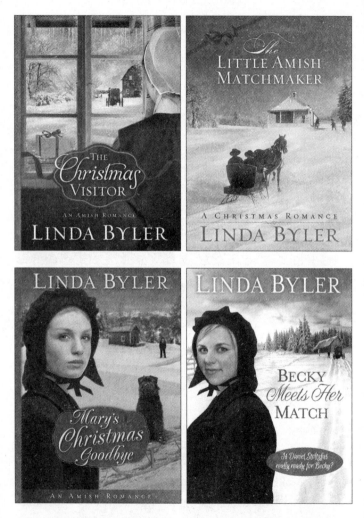

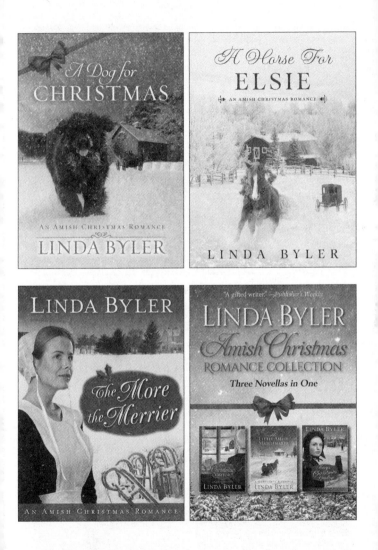

THE HEALING

A SECOND CHANCE

HOPE DEFERRED

LOVE IN UNLIKELY PLACES